HEAVIER THAN WATER

O.R. Gerald Ems

Ems Island Publishing

Π1738551

Acknowledgements
I wish to thank my niece Charlotte Hollenberg for her
unfailing
patience in reading the evolving ideas for this book. My
thanks
also for Margaret DeClerk for all artwork and Nick Lester for
his
critical proofreading.

"Right, but what does it say?"

"The approximate distance to the horizon in miles above sea level is the square root of feet multiplied by one and a half."

"Clever boy, and you picked up the approximate."

"Well, that's what you wrote. How approximate is it?"

"Better than 99%."

"That seems very close. Where did the formula come from?" from the boy, ever curious.

"It's called the Pythagorean principle, developed by the Greek philosopher Pythagoras over two thousand years ago."

"It's to do with triangles. I believe that you'll learn it next year in the eighth grade."

"So how far is the horizon from the Marina?"

"How high would your eyes be above the water level?"

"It changes based on the tide."

"Right. Let's say the average tide."

"The dock is about 8 feet above the water, my eyes are four feet above that, and if I stand on the bench another 2 feet."

"So, about 14 feet?"

"Yes."

"OK, 14 feet multiplied by one and a half is 21. You did square roots a couple of years ago, so what is the square root of 21?"

"My phone says it's about 4.5, so the horizon I can see from here is about four and a half miles."

The father smiled at his son's use of the phone as a calculator, thinking back to his time as a student when it was logarithms or a slide rule.

"Again, clever boy."

"I get it from my father," this said with a smile.

"Not really. Your mother is the smart one in this family."

The boy just nodded and smiled in agreement.

"How far can you see from the Concorde?" asked the boy being fascinated by supersonic flight.

"Umm, let me see. I think the Concorde cruised at about 60,000 feet."

"What is one and a half times that?"

"90,000 feet," replied the boy without hesitation, pulling out his phone to complete the calculation.

The father stopped him. "Let's do this the old-fashioned way."

"We need the square root of 90,000. The easiest way is to say 9 times 10,000. What is the number multiplied by itself which equals 9?"

Again, with no hesitation, "Three."

"How many zeroes after the 1 in 10,000?"

"Four."

"And the square root of four?"

"Two."

"So, then you get a 1 followed by two zeroes, which is 100, multiplied by 3 which is 300."
"So you at 60,000 feet can see 300 miles in every direction. High enough to see the curvature of the earth."

"Yes," said the boy, "exactly like the Concorde poster in my room."

As he was back standing on the bench at fourteen feet above sea level, he calculated that the yacht, more like a small sailboat than a yacht, was four and a half miles away, though he worked out that you could see the top of the mast when it was a few miles further away. He noticed it was almost high tide with very little wind. The boat did not show any sails, so it was coming in on its motor, which meant about an hour to dock. He would start videotaping it in about half an hour.

Today he decided to walk from his parent's house on Mast Mall, just across the creek that separated it from the Marina Del Rey beach. On other days, depending on his mood, he either cycled or used his in-line skates.

Apart from the incoming boat, it had been, like

many others, a slow morning. As usual, very few boats ever left their docking station. He got hungry early and took one of the sandwiches that his aunt had prepared for him. It was one of his favorites, sardines, and tomato on rye bread.

He was amused by all the corporate types in suits and ties who came pouring out of the nearby Hyatt hotel, assuming, from the plastic name tags they were wearing, that they were attending a convention inside the hotel.

While both of his parents were in London, his aunt was looking after him, not babysitting, as he hated the word.

He had told his parents that at twelve years old, he did not need to be looked after. While they agreed he was mature for his age, being an only child to a couple in their early fifties, they would be charged with child abuse if they left him alone at his age.

"How would people know?" he asked.

"They would for sure. There are always tattletales around."

"What are tattletales?"

"Those are people who delight in exposing to the authorities even the most minuscule infractions."

"OK, anyway I like Aunt Edna,"

And so it came to pass that his Aunt Edna, a retired school principal, was looking after him for the summer. She was happy to escape the summer heat of Phoenix, so it worked out well for everybody.

Her only rules for the boy were, "Don't do anything stupid, and let me know where you are at all times."

The boy thought that both his parents were geniuses, as they both were doctors, but he was confused as they never saw patients. His father, Dr. John Hampstead, explained to him, that "his mother, Dr. Mirna Hampstead, and he had doctorates in molecular biology and economics respectively, and that doctors who had patients were doctors of medicine."

"How did that happen?" asked his son.

"Here is the five-cent tour," replied his father. "I was born and grew up in El Paso Texas, a completely bilingual, English and Spanish city."

"I then went to The University of Northern Arizona in Flagstaff, which I thought was the coldest place on earth after El Paso. I studied math and physics as I was good at them. After I graduated, I wanted to go to business school but also wanted to do something different."

"What was that?"

"All the people I knew wanted to go to the Wharton School of Business school, but I applied and was accepted by the INSEAD Business School, just outside Paris."

"Did you know that I also speak French?"

"Say something in French."

"*Bonjour mon fils comment ça va?* which is, hello my son, how are you?"

"Cool. Where did you learn it?"

"My mother, your grandmother, was born in Paris and came to the US when she was twelve. She missed speaking French, and when I was growing up, only spoke to me in French, so I got fluent in the language. INSEAD wanted three languages, so I was fine with English, French, and Spanish."

"You know your grandmother wants you to spend next summer at her house on the Normandy coast."

"That would be great, but I don't speak any French."

"*Pas de problème.* We'll solve that in the coming year."

CHAPTER TWO

I finished my run around the Hollywood reservoir. 'Run' was a most generous description. Huff, puff, amble, and shamble would be more accurate. Where had the football jock who could run the 40-yard dash in under 5 seconds gone? At that time, I weighed a buck fifty. Right now, it was more like two bucks and change. I hadn't lost any weight since I started to run, which disappointed me, but on the other hand, my waist size had gone down from 40 to 38 inches. Maybe it was fat converting to muscle.

I was surprised when my cell phone rang with the tone of my long-time assistant/secretary/office manager/general factotum, Dolores. We had an unwritten rule that she would never call me on my runs.

"Dolores, is something wrong?"

"There's a lady to see you, says it's most urgent."

"Tell her be there in about 45 minutes after I shower and change."

"She asks if you could come sooner."

"Only if she is ok with me being sweaty and in running gear."

"She is flying back to Seattle early afternoon, so even in your present condition, now would be most appreciated. I drove back to the office in my near-pristine BMW model 3 convertible." I used to take my Suzuki motorcycle to the reservoir for my runs, but I stopped after someone who wanted my parking space had punted the motorcycle down into the ravine below, causing much aggravation and a sizable repair bill. Lester and Barker had two assigned parking spaces at their West LA office. I let Dolores use one for her Cadillac CT6, which she had nicknamed "shrimpy" referring to her love and ownership of Cadillac land yachts of yore, of which the last of the finned behemoth had finally expired. To her the CT6, which was considerably larger than my BMW, was tiny. The benefit of the CT6 to me was her ability to fit it into one parking space. The land yachts required to be parked diagonally across two spaces.

As I passed my office towards the parking structure where I had a monthly parking place, at a usurious $390/month, I noticed a Toyota Camry in the visitor space. I slowly walked the three blocks back from the parking place to my office to let myself cool off.

Dolores greeted me at the door to the office. "It's a Josie Pedersen, don't know if Mrs. or Miss, but a very nice lady. I knew you wouldn't mind if I put her in your office. I gave her a coffee and some cookies from your secret stash."

She smirked as she referred to my snacking on these cookies as the cause of my increased weight.

Mrs. or Miss Pedersen (it turned out to be 'miss' even though she had been married) was pacing my office. She was a very attractive fiftyish underneath a mousy set of clothes and very little makeup, and had the bluest eyes I had ever seen. They were so blue that I even suspected that she was wearing colored contact lenses. From her slim build, I suspected ~~that~~ she was very athletic.

I greeted her and apologized for the wait.

"I understand that Dolores has been looking after you."

"Very well. She's a sweetheart and even found me these delicious orange cream cookies."

Just hearing the description of my secret stash made my mouth water, but scarfing down a bunch of them would defeat the purpose of my morning run.

"How did you hear about me?"

"Jerollee Roberts. I understand that you did some delicate sleuthing for her recently, with which she was very happy. I also did some research on you and found that you had solved a couple of complicated murder cases. I decided you are the person for me."

"So, what can I do for you?"

"It's about my twin sister, Joyce. According to the police and the Medical Examiner, she died by drowning, but I believe there is more to it. I suspect foul play, almost certainly by her husband Michael Broadmoor."

"Money is no problem," she added.

I just nodded and told her I would start looking into the problem immediately, but I needed more information.

"What is your sister's full name?"

"Joyce Broadmoor."

"Are you identical twins?"

"Monozygotic all the way," which I took as a yes.

"Do they have any children?"

"Yes, they have three, two boys fifteen and twelve years old, and a girl fourteen years old. Frankly, I was surprised as I assumed Michael would be a terrible father, but I was wrong. The boys, Kent and Doug, adore him, but I don't know why they hate their mother. The daughter, Suzy, is the opposite. She loves her mother and hates her father."

"The two boys take very much after Michael. Both are brilliant at science, particularly the younger son who is on the autistic spectrum and is approaching genius. He could be smarter than his father. Suzi, the daughter, is musically also a near genius, and has already composed pieces that are being played by a major orchestra."

"Sorry for all that information. It's probably

irrelevant to what happened to my sister."

"No apologies required. You can never have too much information."

"What about work?"

"My sister ran a very successful building supply company. Our father, an immigrant from Sweden, opened the company with a small store which he felt was a contrast to the big national chains. When he died, we were up to three stores with a value of about fifteen million dollars."

"Who inherited the stores?"

"We did jointly. Joyce always loved the stores and had worked there in all kinds of roles since graduating with a business degree from USC. I had less than zero interest, so she offered to buy my 50% share at $750,000/year for 10 years."

"She insisted that I keep a 20% ownership and a seat on the board with profit sharing. She was the most generous person."

"What is the value of the business now?"

"Since our father died nine years ago, Joyce has expanded to twelve stores, each one less than 5,000 square feet. Several of the big chains have made offers of around a hundred million to buy her out."

"Sorry to be indelicate, but who inherits?"

"Probably Michael. I'll send you her lawyer's information."

"I sense that you aren't fond of her husband?"

"He's a truly brilliant genius in all kinds of chemistry, but an arrogant prick with the social grace of a malevolent skunk. His favorite greeting to his fellow workers was 'hey shit-for-brains.'"

"Ouch, did your sister agree with your description of Michael?"

"Not when they met. Michael could be a real charmer, but that lasted only into the first few months of marriage. After that, he reverted to his true colors."

"Why not divorce him?"

"We don't do that in our family," adding as an aside that she had divorced her first and only husband after a couple of years.

"We were both high-powered attorneys working for the same multinational law firm. We were too similar, and, in the end, that proved unworkable."

"Tell me more about Michael Broadmoor."

"The man is brilliant, truly brilliant. Things went quite well as he obtained his degrees from Stanford and UC Berkeley. The problems began when he started working. Apparently, he's quite charming in job interviews. As soon as he started working, everyone that interacted around him wanted to quit or be transferred. As far as the companies were concerned, it was either getting rid of Michael or losing most of their staff. The choice was obvious, so they laid him off with a generous separation package."

"So, what happened?"

"Joyce tried to help. She leased a place in the City of Industry. The space was a former lab, so it had all the utilities, one pull emergency shower over every workspace, fume hoods, etc. She hired a really good lab director and lab techs. It all fell apart as all staff left within a month. As I said, Michael treated everyone else as complete idiots, but he also was terrible at all other aspects of the lab."

"So where is he now?"

"Joyce made him VP of forward planning for the company. She gave him a nice office and a salary of $250,000/year.

As far as he was concerned it was "thanks for the pocket money."

"Does he do any planning?"

"No, nor is he expected to. He has no staff and spends his time reading lots of chemistry-related literature. He is now a well-regarded theoretical chemist and, as Joyce told me, has written some important articles."

"So, it wasn't all sweetness and light?"

"Not really. Michael wanted to live the high life. He grumbled that their six-bedroom house on the Venice canals was a peasant's house and wanted one of the 'castles' in the Hollywood hills where he could rub shoulders with all 'the beautiful people.'"

"She also allowed him to buy a Ferrari as his company car, which she thought looked garish beside her midnight blue Bentley convertible."

"This was also a source of friction. Even though it was a company car, she would not allow him to drive it to the corporate headquarters in Culver City, the site of their first store. They moved the old store to a bigger site a block away."

"As I said, she wouldn't allow him to drive the Ferrari to work, but insisted that he went with his old Toyota Camry. She used an old Honda Accord to the office and was driven from there to all their other locations."

"No doubt her death and subsequent inheritance would allow him to live the high life that he craved."

"That is exactly my suspicion." She emphasized the 'is.'

Armed with that information, I said my goodbyes to Josie Pedersen and assured her I would pursue the case, if indeed there was one.

CHAPTER THREE

The boy had just finished his sandwich when he got a text message from his friend, Trevor.

"Hey BB fancy a spot of lunch?"

Trevor was his best friend. BB stood for "Ben bro" for the two considered themselves more than best friends and thought of each other as a brother 'bro.'

Trevor had been born in the US and had lived his whole life in California, but he loved using British phrases learned from his British parents hence 'a spot of lunch.'

Even though Bren, short for Brendan, had finished his lunch, he answered, "TB, for sure, whadya fancy?"

"Burgers in Venice?"

"Works for me."

"On your bike?" Trevor knew Brendan varied his journeys to the Marina Boat Basin between walking, biking, and inline skates.

"No, on foot."

"K, see you at your place in thirty."

If Brendan had said bike, Trevor would have met him at the Marina.

Brendan was average for his age, at five feet in height and ninety pounds in weight. Trevor, only three months older was six inches taller and a good thirty pounds heavier. Brendan was as thin as a stick and Trevor was much bulkier. Neither had an ounce of fat on them, being constantly on the move, mainly with sports.

Brendan was just arriving at his house when Trevor cycled up. He was on his new, to him, super-duper Santa Cruz Hightower Carbon S Mountain Bike. He had bought it only a few weeks ago on eBay, still in its shipping container for $1,000, much less than the retail price of $5,199. They both wondered if it was a stolen item, but the price was so good that Trevor went for it.

This was a lot of money for Trevor. Both his father and grandfather promised him that they would each chip in one-third of the price if he was able to save the remaining third. He did so by working a collection of jobs, sometime around the clock.

"Give me five minutes," said Brendan, who owned a pedestrian middle-of-the-road mountain bike, perfectly adequate for the riding he did. There was no way he was going to accompany Trevor on the crazy mountain bike trails, almost all of single and double black diamonds. Brendan was happy with a nice green-level cruising trail.

"Cool."

Trevor lived nearby on Outrigger mall, so it had taken him less than a minute to cycle to Brendan's house. Together they cycled over the pedestrian bridge separating their homes from Speedway, went one more block to the sidewalk that was Ocean Front Walk, made a right, and cruised slowly to Washington Boulevard. There they picked up the Venice beach bicycle path, slaloming around the pedestrians who were either ignorant or unmindful of the 'no pedestrians' rule on the bike path. They had to be careful as overnight the wind had piled sand on the bike path which made the going a little treacherous. Not so for Trevor. He attacked every pile of sand as a sliding obstacle to be overcome.

They made small talk as they passed Muscle Beach on their left and the shops selling seaside paraphernalia on their right. They made a right turn onto Rose Street to the Win-Dow Café.

Brendan stayed with the bikes while Trevor got their food, a single cheeseburger for Brendan. He was not that hungry, having already eaten a sandwich. He washed down the cheeseburger with lemonade. Trevor was all over a double cheeseburger and coke. They went back the short distance to Venice beach and found an empty bench where they slowly ate and let the sun wash over them.

"So, what do you hear from your parents, the Doctors Hampstead?"

Trevor knew that Brendan and his parents had a WhatsApp conversation most days.

"They moved out of their hotel. They very much wished to live in Hampstead, the Hampsteads from Hamstead, which is in Northwest London. They found it 'a little pricey' even with both their housing allowances, so they settled for a furnished 'flat' which is what the Brits call an apartment, in Chalk Farm near the underground station, which is what the Londoners call their subway. It's still easy for them to get to Hampstead, which is only two stops further north on the Northern Line, and equally easy for them to get to LSE and University College London, which is where his father and mother were based, respectively.

His Dad added, "we wanted to have enough money so that we can do other things such as plays and even the open-air concerts on Hampstead Heath. This weekend we are taking the Eurostar to Paris for a few days."

"Loved that train," said Trevor as he and his family had been to Europe the previous year.

"Did my dad tell you the Eurostar story of when they were in Paris in 1995?" asked Brendan

"No."

They were staying in Paris, which my dad knew well. This time they took the Eurostar to London. The train shot down from Paris to Calais at 300 K (km/hour) flew through the 30-plus miles long Euro Tunnel to Ashford in Kent, and then chugged the sixty-odd miles to London at a leisurely seventy miles per hour. It took as long to go the sixty miles from Ashford to London as the time for the three hundred kilometers from Paris to Calais.

"It only took us just over two hours" Trevor observed.

"Yea that's right. After Dad told me the story, I looked it up on the Internet. They did not complete the high-speed link from Ashford to London until 2007. That alone took about 40 minutes off the travel time."

They finished their hamburgers, and pushing their bikes walked slowly along the Venice Beachfront neither of them being in a hurry to be anywhere.

"What exactly are your parents doing in London?"

"Well, dad is at the London School of Economics. You know he works in a think-tank in Santa Monica modeling government responses to catastrophic events. He has been invited as a Senior Visiting Fellow to LSE to go over his experience with modeling and compare it with his European peers."

"Sounds high-powered."

"He's a high-powered kind of guy."

"And your mom?"

"It's some complicated DNA thing. She tried to explain to me, but it was way over my head."

"I understood that she is part of what they call a 'hammer group' that University College London put together from grants from EMBO and the Welcome Trust. The idea is that they bring worldwide experts together for a short time to hammer away at a problem. I did pick up that it's to do with mitochondrial and chloroplastal mutations, whatever that is."

"It sounds even more complicated. You're lucky to have such smart parents."

"Yeah. Sometimes I wish they were not so, as it would be easier for me."

Just then Trevor's cell phone beeped with a text.

"It's my dad. They just rented a house in Tahoe for a month. You're invited."

"Fantastic. When do we leave?"

"Tomorrow. We're taking the Chevy Tahoe so we can carry the bikes."

Not the Hampsteads in Hamstead thought Brendan, but the Tahoe to Tahoe.

CHAPTER FOUR

Josie Pedersen was true to her word. Less than two hours after we concluded our meeting I received a message. "Our accountant, Grant Chester, can meet you at 10 a.m. tomorrow and included a Culver City address. He has no problem giving you information on the will, as he is filing it with the court on Monday." When I looked at the address on Google maps I saw that it was only three blocks from the Winslow Building Supplies headquarters.

I got there some thirty minutes early. Not only was I concerned about finding a parking space but noted on the Google map that there was a Starbucks almost across the street. It turned out that there was convenient off-street parking right next door to Starbucks. I sipped my coffee and read the headlines on my phone.

Precisely at 10 am, I rang the bell. I often play a game in my mind, picturing what a person would look like before I met them. With Grant Chester, I wasn't only out of the ballpark, but I also wasn't even on the same planet. I had pictured a middle-aged man, probably overweight, with thick glasses, wearing an ill-fitting suit covered in cigarette ash. I was met by a trim, very fit-looking Asian gentleman, seventy-five years old if he was a day, dressed in an elegantly cut lightweight pale grey suit, with a beautiful silk tie of contrasting blues.

"Mr. Lester?"

"Sorry, I was admiring your tie."

"I'm rather fond of it myself. It's an Ermenegildo Zegna."

I looked it up on the internet when I got home. Priced at $375, it was more than the clothes in my wardrobe were worth.

He shook my hand vigorously. "It's good to meet you, and yes, I know my name is the same as a BBC television series."

I smiled at that and asked him, "How long have you been The Winslow Company accountant?"

"Forever, or at least since old man Pedersen started the business. We had known each other in High School, so it was a kind of mutual support system."

"Why Winslow?"

"I don't know. I suggested Pedersen, but for reasons only known to him he wanted an English-sounding company."

"Once Pedersen died Joyce took over and she started rapidly expanding the business. I recommended that she found a bigger accounting company to handle her business."

She would have none of it. "What was good

enough for my father is good enough for me. Besides that, it would take me ages to bring a new company up to speed. Just hire more people if you need them."

"So, I did just that. My main hire was an accountant specializing in real estate transactions. But you're not here to make small talk so let's get right to it."

"Who gets the estate?"

"On the whole, it goes to Michael Broadmoor. You know that Josie Pedersen, who had returned to her maiden name after she divorced, holds twenty percent of the company."

"Yes, she told me her sister insisted that she keep it."

"Apart from a few small bequests, ten percent of the value of the company goes "pro-rata" based on time of service to all her workers."

"That seems fair."

"Joyce felt that all workers were equal in doing their jobs. As far as she was concerned, a janitor with ten years of service should get ten times more than a Vice President with one year of service. Some long-term employees could get as much as fifty thousand dollars."

"Nice, but not enough for any of them to commit murder."

He raised an eyebrow at my comment but carried on, "Josie told me that Joyce had had offers of around one hundred million for the company. That means that after Josie's twenty percent, and the employees' ten percent, Michael will get about seventy million."

"Not exactly chump change."

"Not even to a billionaire."

"Any life insurance?"

"Only for a million dollars."

To me, a million was a lot more than 'only.'

"Anything else?"

"The house is free and clear. It's probably worth around three mills."

"I forgot to add… there's also ten million in key person insurance."

"What's that?"

"By definition, key person insurance is a life insurance policy that a company purchases on its key executive's lives. The company pays for the plan and gets the payout if a key person dies."

"So, Michael Broadmoor would also get a share of it."
"He probably would get all of it, as he could withdraw it from the company before any sale."

"One way or another, Michael Broadmoor will end up with close to one hundred million dollars."

"Give or take, that would be my conclusion."

"You would stay on through the sale?"

"Unless the board says otherwise. After that, I'm gone. I've only stayed this long as a favor to Joyce Broadmoor."

And with that, I said my thanks to Grant Chester. A hundred million dollars was certainly a motive. People have been killed for a fraction of that.

CHAPTER FIVE

It was clear that my next step had to be the autopsy information. Over the years I have become friendly with Jaqueline Hillsboro, more precisely Dr. Jaqueline Hillsboro MD. Ph.D. the number two in the Medical Examiner's office. She had obtained her MD from Harvard School of Medicine and her Ph.D. in Forensic Science from West Virginia University, an unusual combination that stood her well to becoming director of the department when the current director, Dr. Layla Ibrahim, retired next year. When asked why she went into forensic science after her MD. Dr. Hillsboro answered, "I have no idea, it just appealed to me."

She and I had become friends over the years, finding we enjoyed many common interests. We were always trying to one-up each other with outrageous puns, but most unusual is that we were both crossword fiends. Jaqueline would often tease me about how easy my crosswords were. "A famous racing car make made in the sixties, five letters?"

"Lotus?"

Jaqueline did the crosswords from the English newspapers.

"How do they differ from the US crosswords?"

"OK, here's an easy clue."

"Man backs up entry for building greeter, seven letters."

"Can you work it out?"

"Not a clue."

"Man backs up probably means that it is at the end of the word. That leaves a four-letter word meaning entry."
"How about door?"

"It could work. It would make the whole word, doorman."

"And a doorman greets people. So that was an easy clue?"

"Not easy, super easy."
"So what's your favorite crossword?"

"Times of London Sunday crossword. It's a real stinker."

A couple of days later, I jumped online and looked at one of the Sunday crosswords. Not only could I not answer a single clue, but I also didn't even understand what they were asking. I always thought that Jaqueline was smarter than me, but that strongly cemented that belief.

The good news was that we had arranged to meet that very evening. We alternated as to who chose the restaurant. Last time I had chosen 1 Pico in the Shutters hotel on Santa Monica Beach. I loved the location, and the food wasn't bad either.

This time Jaqueline had chosen Palm Thai near the Capitol Records Building in Hollywood. It was conveniently near her new home on Grace Avenue in the Whitley Heights section of Hollywood. As with all the other surrounding houses, it was a gorgeous Spanish style with a huge purple bougainvillea plant running along the street-facing exterior wall. The garden had grapefruit and orange trees and what Jaqueline described as a "wannabe" banana tree. The house was not large by today's standards but had stunning tile work with floor-to-ceiling windows and doors with semi-circular tops.

Whitley Heights was an area of Mediterranean-style homes built in the 1920s, home to many celebrities in the film industry such as Charlie Chaplin, Rudolf Valentino, Marlene Dietrich, and dozens of other stars, producers, and directors. It was completely spoiled when it was bisected by the Hollywood freeway.

I arrived first at the Palm Thai Restaurantand ordered a large Singha bottle of beer and two glasses. I resisted ordering an appetizer being well aware that Jaqueline could be held up at work. If it had been a serious delay she would have texted me. Ten minutes after the appointed time I decided to risk it and ordered a bowl of Tom Kha, Thai coconut soup, spicy hot, with shrimp. We both liked our food very spicy, so I was on safe ground, getting the soup spicy.

Jaqueline, who he greeted by her full name French style, not Jacks or Jaquie as most people called her, arrived at the same time as the soup. She had told me that the Jaqueline name had come down through generations, even as far back as her family's immigration from France to Quebec Canada in the mid-eighteen hundreds, and subsequently to the United States in the early nineteen hundreds.

She looked stunning in a grey pants suit and pale blue blouse with a beautiful turquoise and silver brooch with a matching bracelet. Her jet-black hair was showing the first hint of silver. Many women looked somewhat frumpy in a pants suit, but not Jaqueline. Like me, she liked to run for exercise, but unlike me did not do that with a ton of excess weight. Hence her slim build.

I always asked her the same question, "how is it that someone as gorgeous and accomplished as you isn't married?"

Always the same answer, "I am, to my work."

We settled into a comfortable silence as we ate their soup, which we followed up with duck Pad Thai. We looked around the restaurant and were amazed that we appeared to be the only couple not on their cell phones. I joked that our fellow diners were not talking, but texting each other across the table.

At the end of the meal, I walked her to a waiting Uber that would take her the short distance to her home.

"I need a small favor."

"Small, as in your usual impossible asks?"

"No really. I need the results of an autopsy on a drowning victim Joyce Broadmoor."

"I'll see what I can do."

With a peck on the cheek, she thanked him for dinner and waved at him from the disappearing Uber.

The next afternoon, I received a text from her. "Autopsy shows classic evidence of drowning with no suspicious circumstances, such as drugs or poisons."

Worth a try, I thought, unsurprised by the result.

CHAPTER SIX

Time for a chat with the police. Unfortunately, I knew no one in the Pacific division. I put in a call to my longtime friend Chris Badinovitch, Captain of Detectives in Beverly Hills.

"Hey John, long time, you must really need something."

"Nice to talk to you, too. I need a favor, but the main reason I called ~~you~~ was to invite you and Jill to the new Indian restaurant on Pico."

"Man, Jill would kill me if we didn't first have dinner at our new home. I'll talk to her to see if she has a free evening."

Jill, Chris's wife, was a newly minted Ph.D. in psychology. She was volunteering some evenings in a homeless shelter in Santa Monica, trying her best to counsel people who, on the whole, were resistant to such help.

"That would be great. By the way, do you know anyone in the Pacific Division?"

"What do you need?"

"A brief chat about the drowning death of a woman named Joyce Broadmoor."

And so it came to pass that I was sitting across

a table from a newly minted wet-behind-the-ears detective Nathan Sharrow. His suit, a purple-brown, no doubt all the rage at his graduation, was dated in size, as it was now tight and a little short in the arms and legs. It did not help that his green and yellow tie screamed mis-harmonization with his suit color. I wondered if he was old enough to shave. His jet-black hair contrasted with a white face that was unusual in suntanned California. There was a ghost of a previous acne infection on his face.

He opened by saying, "I'm only here as a courtesy from my captain to your friend Captain Badass."

"Badinovitch."

"Yeah, that's what I said."

It was clear that he thought of himself as really 'hot shit' and no doubt regarded me just as a retriever (no pun intended) of lost dogs.

"Joyce Broadmoor" and he rattled through all the statistics of date, time of death, incident number, and witnesses in a monotone voice clearly outlining his boredom with me and the entire case file.

"I'm only here because the sister of the dead woman, Josie Pedersen, has hired me to investigate her sister's death. She believes it was murder."

"Makes no difference who hired you. It doesn't change the fact that there are no signs of anything untoward. It was a straight drowning."

He was preening at his use of the word 'untoward.'

"What about the life vest?"

"Duh. We are de-tec-ti-ves." And with each syllable, which he pronounced individually, he pointed to his chest.

"Standard life vest that you can see on hundreds of boats in the marina. It looked as if it had come right out of the showroom."

"Don't you think it improbable that someone drowns wearing a life vest?"

"Improbable yes, highly unusual yes, almost impossible yes, but impossible no. We believe that Mrs. Broadmoor was upended by a large wave and drowned before a second wave pushed her back upright."

Now that's a highly improbable scenario, I thought to myself.

And with an, "I expected some really clever questions from a private dick of your experience," left the room without even a backward glance, leaving me to make my way out of the building.

I came out on Culver Boulevard, near a bunch of three and four stories apartment buildings fronting several fast-food restaurants across the street. I located a Starbucks at the junction of Culver and Washington Boulevard, close enough that I decided to walk, leaving my car in the nearby parking structure.

After I calmed down from the apparent complete lack of interest in this case by the police, I decided to go to the Marina Boat Basin in the vain hope of finding a witness. To what I had no idea, but as they say, 'friction is less than stiction,' so better to keep going than sit on my ass hoping that something helpful would fly in through the window.

I took Washington Boulevard south for the short drive to the marina parking lot, which was mainly empty. I walked along the sidewalk fronting docks A to E and didn't see a soul who looked as if they were working there. Of the few people inside on their boats, no one knew where I might find any of the maintenance people.

Stymied for the moment, I went back to the office where Dolores gave me a stack of messages, none of which were of interest, not even a lost dog. I did routine work, ate an ordered-in sandwich, and kept at it until 4 p.m.

Back to the Marina, the same parking space, retracing my steps of the morning.

This time, as I was passing dock C, I saw someone looking like maintenance. Responding to my shout, he came up to the gate and let me in. I asked if he was maintenance and after affirming that he was, introduced himself as Chip Moreno.

He was about forty with bleached blond hair, and a faded T-shirt from a boat supply company with the slogan 'we have what you want,' which certainly was an offer with unlimited potential. His face, arms, and legs were tanned to a deep mahogany. He told me he had been working here for the last eight years having spent all his working life around boats.

"I grew up and lived in Bellingham, Washington State, working on boats since I was sixteen, in and out of the San Juan Islands. I moved here as I wanted a dryer climate, as I got arthritis and the damp up there hurt me."

After a little more chit-chat, I asked him if the boat belonging to the Broadmoors was here.

"No boat belonging to the Broadmoors here. Do you mean the one belonging to the Marshalls that Mrs. Broadmoor drowned on?"

"Yes, that's what I meant."

"That's slip B 1050, but they aren't there now. You can usually catch them in the evening as they like to have a glass of wine watching the sunset."

"Did you see the Marshall's boat come in?"

"No, but you should talk to the kid."
"Kid?"

"Yeah, haven't seen him for a few days, but he's usually here filming all the boats going in and out. Told me he did moving collages of the boats, whatever the fuck that is. Puts them on his Facebook page. He gave me his Facebook page information."

"Do you still have it?"

"Probably in my jacket pocket. Follow me."
I followed him to a slip on dock D.

"Wait here." He came back up from the boat a few minutes later with a slip of paper with the Facebook information.

The page did not have his name, but did have some contact information.

"Did he give you his name?"

"I think it was Brandon."

"Do you live on your boat?"

"Oh no, this isn't mine. Lots of the owners like somebody around at night. I have about twenty boats that I rotate around, sleeping a few nights on each. It's a lot better than my three hundred square foot shoebox that I rent for eleven hundred bucks in West LA. Anyway, I sleep much better on a boat than on land."

With a wave of thanks, I left him and went back to the office.

CHAPTER SEVEN

I got back to the Marina about thirty minutes before sunset. I asked Chip how to get into the slips as access to the boats was via locked gates. He told me to text him, so after parking, I did just that when I was about one hundred yards from the gate entry to dock B. Chip was at the gate before I even got there.

"I knew you would arrive about now," he said as he escorted me to slip B1050. As Chip had told me, the Marshalls were sitting on deck chairs, wine glasses in hand.

"Mr. and Mrs. Marshall, this is Mr. Lester I told you about."

"Hello, we're Twain and Polly."
"John."

They brought out another deck chair.

"Chardonnay OK?"

"Great" and with that, they gave me a large glass of what tasted like a very good wine.

"Let's talk later." And with that, we settled into an amiable silence until the sun had fully set below the horizon.

My immediate impression was how nice the

Marshalls were. They were small, he at five foot six, she at a shade under five feet. They were both retired. He was a pharmacist, and she had been a nurse. They told me they never made that much money. It was clear that they had managed their finances well having sent their two children through college.

I wondered how they got on with such a miserable person as Michael Broadmoor.

It was as if Twain had read my mind.

"You want to know about the Broadmoors?" Twain asked.

"They were a great couple, especially just after they married."

"Have you known them for a long time?"

"Nearly forever. Our daughter and Joyce were in the same class at high school. Michael, we only got to know when Joyce married. Michael was a charmer when he wanted something, and that something was sailing with us. He was a really good sailor, much better than us. He wanted his own boat, but Joyce wasn't willing to splurge for one. We were the next best thing."

"He also taught the two boys how to sail, and they are both terrific sailors. They often come out with us at weekends and school holidays."

"I also heard he's a real charmer, at least enough that he managed to charm a Ferrari out of his wife.'"

"There's an interesting story to that. Tom Dickinson is a major supplier to Josie's company. After making a sales call, he took Michael out to lunch. Considering Michael's temperament, it was amazing that they got on, but they did. At lunch, Tom mentioned he was going on to the Ferrari dealership to order a car."

"At this, Michael suggested he go along. Long story short, they were told that they could get a really good discount if they bought two."

"He persuaded Josie, and she agreed. They were going through a rough patch, and she felt it would ease things. The two cars are identical, even to the license plates, except that Tom's license plate number ends with a seven, and Michael's with a one."

"Do remember the plate numbers?" I asked.

"Not really. I do remember that they both started P888. I was surprised that Michael did not get a vanity plate as he has on his other car."

"Vanity plate?"

"Yes. Michael told me it was an alchemist's dream."

"Making gold out of lead."

"That's it. I remember the plate number on his other car. PB N2 AU."

"Lead into gold."

"Coincidently, Tom Dickinson and his wife were also on the boat when Josie died."

We continued to chat, and they told me how they scrimped and saved to get their kids through college. They were also smart enough, thirty-five years ago, to have bought a house on Frey Avenue, just off Washington Boulevard on the Venice side, before prices had spiked to an unaffordable level.

"Our boat, a Catalina 30, is our only indulgence. We bought it when our daughter graduated from college, finding ourselves with a little spare money. We love watching the sunset from here. It's easy as we live close by and often walk."

I asked them why they had named their boat 'A brief affair?'

"The previous owner, a lingerie salesman, named it. It's a play on words, 'brief' being a form of underwear."

"We liked the name, so we kept it." He went on to tell me the changes and extras they had added to the boat.

"Sorry John, I'm rambling on. You came to talk about Joyce's unfortunate drowning."

"Yes, thanks. Her twin sister Josie asked me to look into it. So far it looks like an accident but drowning while wearing a life vest seemed a little unusual."

"It was, we were all very upset, especially Michael when we got her back to the boat."

"Was it unusual for her to sit on the stern and fall off?"

"It happened often enough that Michael gave her an air horn to sound when she fell off. He also made her a bracelet that activated a light beacon if it got wet."

"So did you turn around as soon as you heard the horn go off?"

"We didn't hear the horn," Polly told me. "I noticed she wasn't on the stern. We had just done hardtack to port. Michael brought the boat as quickly as he could."

Twain took over the narrative. "We went back to where we thought she would be."

"How long would that have been?"

"Somewhere between five and ten minutes."

"And she was floating in the water?"

"No, we made a big circle and when we came back to the same spot, we saw the flashing light beacon. Normally she waved at us, laughing as we came to pick up her up."

"Not this time?"

"No, she was slumped over. Michael immediately dove in and helped bring her onto the deck. It was clear that she was gone."

"Even though that was the case, Michael removed her life vest and Polly tried CPR for several minutes. He called the Coast Guard. They were there in about twenty minutes. They concluded that there was nothing they could do, so they escorted us back to the coastguard slip. An ambulance and the police were waiting for us."

"Did you feel it was strange that she had drowned?"

"Absolutely. Michael was distraught and kept on saying 'this is impossible' over and over again."

"That's all I can tell you."

I weaved back to my car, having consumed a second large chardonnay they pushed on me.

What did I have?

The autopsy showed a straightforward drowning with no signs of foul play or drugs.

The description of the accident by the Marshalls seemed to be straightforward.

The Facebook page by 'Brandon' showed some interesting technical wizardry by having boats spinning on their axes, line dancing, and playing leapfrog, but nothing showing a boat being met by the police.

Once again, what did I have? The simple answer was zip, nada, nothing.

In the classic, 'motive, means and opportunity' I certainly had a motive, opportunity maybe, but means, if indeed it was murder, completely eluded me.

At irregular intervals, three of us in the detective business would meet and exchange information techniques and any other items of interest. Apart from me, there was CT who did a lot of legwork for my agency, and the third person of our trio was Issy Bisikudoft, usually called Issy Bissy, either as a name, statement, or question. CT was dressed in his usual uniform of jeans and a t-shirt, which always sported a children's cartoon character. Today it was the roadrunner with his characteristic 'beep beep.'

Issy on the other hand was elegant as always in a lightweight pale beige suit, white shirt, and equally pale grey tie. He always dressed this way except when on a job. He could dress so that he literally disappeared into the woodwork. I had seen him enter clubs and restaurants where not a single person noticed him, a talent I wished I possessed.

Today the restaurant was CT's choice, so we met at Ye Olde King's Head near the beach in Santa Monica. We were predictable and homogenous in our choice of full English breakfast washed down with a pint of bitter.

When the meal came, CT pointed to my plate, itemizing the bacon, sausage, friend tomatoes, mushrooms, baked beans, and fried egg, with a finger pointing at my stomach.

"Nice diet."

"It's diet-free blue moon day."

"It's not a blue moon."
"I know, but I missed the last one, so I'm making up for lost time."

"I don't think Juliette would agree with you."

Juliette was my new, and I hoped long-term girlfriend who was trying to put me on a sensible weight loss diet.

After the usual chit-chat, I asked Issy what he was working on. At this point in our relationship, we freely exchanged confidential information, as we trusted each other to keep such information to ourselves.
"Nothing much. I have this guy asking me to find a kid from the Marina."

"What's your client's name?"

"Michael Broadmoor."

At this, all the gods of coincidence clanged in my head at the same time.

"No way! I'm looking into the same guy for a client. She suspects him of murdering his wife."

Both CT and Issy looked at me with disbelief.

"Why did he ask you to find the boy?"

"Said he saw him filming in the Marina. Said he was part of a group developing young talent in the film world."

"Sounds a little thin."

"That's what I thought. But a paying client is a paying client."

"Cannot be the same guy."

"Do you have a photo of the kid?" I asked Issy, as I had tried to contact the kid through Facebook with no luck.

He pulls out his phone and finds a picture of a skinny kid standing on a bench near the Marina Apartments. There is a bicycle leaning against the bench, a backpack next to his feet, and binoculars around his neck. He appears to be shooting with a fancy video camera.

"Michael Broadmoor gave you this picture?"

"Yep, sent to me as an attachment."

Issy blew up the picture to full magnification to get a better look at the boy, but none of us recognized him.

"What about his gear?" asked CT.

Issy then scrolled through various parts of the photo.

"Go back to the backpack," I asked him. "What kinds of boots are those?"

They were partially hidden behind the backpack. At full zoom, half the sole of one boot could be seen.

"That's a soccer boot. My nephew plays and I often take him to games." This from CT.

Issy and I decided to work together to track down the kid. As CT had some knowledge of the soccer scene, he readily accepted that he would ask around at the various soccer venues for youth soccer in the local area.

CHAPTER EIGHT

It took a while for CT to get back to me. It gave me time to attend to some of my other work, mainly routine tracing of people for those who had lost touch, often from school or college days.

"I found one trainer who recognized Brandon from the photo. He asked one of the coaches, who thought his family name was James or Jameson."

"Do you know how many people have those names just in the West LA area?"

Before I could answer, "dozens."

It was a lot easier in the old days when 'You could let your fingers do the walking' by using a telephone directory. Today, if you know how to navigate for information, everything is online. Unfortunately, many people no longer have landlines, with no easy way to find contact numbers from cell phone companies.

CT seemed to have cultivated contacts with those companies. It took him several days to come up with a list of potential possible families. You just can't call and ask if you have a son called Brandon who plays soccer.

"Who is this, and why do you want to know?"

CT came up with a plausible scenario that

his nephew, who played soccer, had met Brandon playing soccer but lost his contact information. While being a little thin, the question had worked, but had not turned up any soccer players.

"Not only don't we have the right name, but I'm an idiot," I told CT.

"I just remembered that when I was talking to Chip, the maintenance guy in the Marina, he told me that Brandon did not always use a bicycle."

"Sometimes he had those things that were like roller skates but with only two wheels. Other times he walked."

"You're talking about in-line skates. That, and the walking, suggests that he must live within walking distance."

CT agreed and told me he would make another circuit of the soccer fields. It took him a few more days but came back with two names, Brendan not Brandon, Brendan Huppermeyer, and Brendan Hampstead, and addresses for both of them.

"You take Huppermeyer, and I'll take Hampstead."

"It's not the Huppermeyer kid" CT texted me, "too old."

The next morning, I went to the address at Mast Court in Marina Del Rey. A lady of about sixty years old answered the door. I introduced myself as a private detective and asked if a Brendan lived there and did some video shooting of the boats.

"There have been thefts from boats, and I am clutching at straws. I was hoping to talk to him about anything he may have seen or photographed."

The lady, who told me she was Edna Hampstead, confirmed that it indeed was her nephew Brendan who took videos of the boats. She was a slim, tall lady with an erect bearing, looking very comfortable in her casual clothes. I could easily believe that she had been a school principal, a fact that she told me later.

"Why don't you come in?"

She offered me a cup of coffee, which I accepted. I sensed she was glad of some company.

There are times when you are instantly comfortable with another person, and despite our generational gap, this was one of those times. We started exchanging some background. She told me that she had lived and taught English in Japan for a few years. I told her of my experience there while in the US Navy. We both loved our time in Japan and swapped stories about the uniqueness of the country. We then reminisced about Europe.

"What are your favorite places in Europe?"

Her answer was Florence and Tuscany. "How about you, John?"

We had long gone past family names.

"This may sound funny, but small French

villages at dinner times. I love the relaxed café culture and going to the restaurant area, usually on the main square, and browsing all the menus displayed outside, from the 'menu fixe' to the specials of the day, side-by-side restaurants trying to outdo each other."

I asked her about her nephew Brendan.

"Unfortunately, he's not here. He's with his friend Trevor's family at Lake Tahoe."

She saw the disappointment on my face.

"I could give him a call and see if he can talk to you."

I left her my card with thanks.

She called me later that day. After exchanging a little chit-chat, she gave me Brendan's cell phone number, recommending that I call him at about 7 p.m.

"I told him all about you."

"Many thanks for your help."
"My pleasure."

I reached out to Brendan that evening and told him my boat theft 'story.'

"Over what period?" Brendan asked me.

"The last three months," I told him.

"That's a lot of video files, really too many to send you."

"I understand. When are you back in LA?"

"Not for another month."
"Ouch. I was hoping to examine them much sooner than that."

"You would have to come up here to do that."

"That would be OK with you?"

"Sure. My aunt said you were an OK person."

"How about Tuesday evening, two days from now?"

"Yeah OK, I'll text you the address."

I decided I would book a motel in Truckee, which could serve as my base, and which was an easy drive to Tahoe Village. I left at six a.m., which I hoped was early enough to avoid the perpetual traffic jams of the LA area. I was going out of LA, which was against the major traffic flow. I worked my way over to the 405 and then picked up I 80 north. Not a traffic holdup in sight. I was soon cruising at 79 miles per hour in the 75 MPH speed limit. As all speedometers on cars read one or two miles per hour high, probably to protect car manufacturers from being sued for false speeding claims, I reckoned I was only two or three miles above the speed limit, definitely not speeding ticket country. As I passed an area about one hundred miles north of Los Angeles, I thought it was ironic that many years earlier I got a speeding ticket around here, doing 66 in what was then a ludicrous speed limit of 55 MPH, so slow that I kept on nodding off, and needed copious amounts of coffee to keep me awake.

After a leisurely mid-morning breakfast in Los Banos, then fighting the traffic around Sacramento I arrived in Truckee just before 3 p.m. and found The Hampton Inn at only $133 non-weekend price.

I had time to spare, so I drove along the lakefront both in California and Nevada. In the main, the houses were large with private boat slips, and what looked like pricy boats moored at many of them. Inevitably I landed in a Starbucks, this one at Incline Village, where I sat in the small outdoor space watching the privileged strolling by with their shopping bags adorned with the names of expensive shops and boutiques.

I returned to the Hampton Inn, spruced up a bit, and made my way to the Tahoe Village address Edna Hampstead had given me.

"They rented a cottage on the lakefront in Tahoe Village."

When I got to the address I was confused. I knew it was the right place as the black Tahoe parked outside had a license plate 'SKITIME' which Brendan had told me was the license plate of Trevor's family car. On the back was a Küat bike carrier with its gold accent. Tied to it was what appeared to be some very fancy mountain bikes.

My confusion stemmed from the description

'cottage,' as this was a house of at least four thousand square feet. It was only a cottage by the fact the entire structure was wood.

I rang the bell, which was immediately opened by a couple of young boys, presumably Brendan and Trevor, confirmed when they introduced themselves. They were alone, Trevor's parents enjoying a glass of wine at a nearby neighbor's house.

"John Lester," I said, a fact that they already knew. They took me to a room, about the size of my apartment, which they called a study. Brendan showed me his computer setup, which was a Microsoft Surface Pro 7 attached to a 40-inch monitor.

"Aren't you worried about your computer, noticing the open doors to the outside?"

"No. When we go out, I replace it with my old Surface Pro 5. I use it to back up the 7, with all my files on the SD drive copied onto it. Before you say it, all my important files are in a 'protected folder' software.

He opened the app, and it came up with 'password hint: national Bird'

"Whose national bird?" I asked him.

"Well, that's a funny story. I went with Dad to a conference he was attending in Uruguay. We were in a Suites Hotel, in the very nice area of Positos in Montevideo, but at night there were all those car alarms. They were all the same with a sequence of sounds, 'ee, ee, ee, iah, iah, iah, honk, honk, honk, bam, bam, bam' repeated over and over."

"The problem was that any noisy car, motorcycle, or truck going by would set off the alarms as most of the motion detectors for the alarms were set too low.

My dad joked that the car alarm was the national bird of Uruguay.

"Dad, if all the cars have the same alarm sounds, it's like having no alarms."

Dad agreed, "ok slugger can you do better?"

"When I got back home, me and Trev, oops, sorry mom, Trev and I thought about it and came up with the idea of no sound but instead have a powerful strobe light. There would be no doubt which car was being broken into. At the same time, it would call the cell phone of the car owner, and if there was GPS built into the car would also send the GPS coordinates."

"We did this with built-in, pre-paid phones if required."

I was intrigued. "What did your dad think?"

"He liked it well enough for us to fix up his car with this. We've now made about twenty cars. We charge $200 plus parts. Some of this money helped Trev buy his fancy bike."

I liked the idea. "Could you do my car? it's a Beemer 3 series convertible."

"For sure."

"How about an ignition cutoff?"

"Not required. We found that the battery pulse required by the strobe affected the ignition so that the car won't start."
"How about a motorcycle?"

"We've done one. You probably guessed that with motorcycles, the problem is someone spraying the strobe and blocking the light."

I had thought no such thing, but kept my ignorance of the issue to myself.
"Trev solved that. He's really smart."
This from a twelve-year-old boy with an IQ probably twice mine.

"Trev found this super polished piece of curved glass with so high a finish, it's called a "molecular polish," that paint just rolls off it. We place it above the strobe light on the motorcycle.

"That's the story of the password" and with that entered a password of at least 20 characters, hidden from me, which Brendan explained was the name of a very obscure car alarm company.

When opened, the protected folder revealed dozens of files.

"I'm afraid I misled you. I just need the file for the day that the lady was drowned."

"So, you're not looking into thefts from boats."

"Sorry, no. I have been hired to look into her death."

"That's OK, I was surprised when you said thefts, as I never saw anything like that."

He then copied that day's file onto a USB stick I had brought with me.

I returned to my hotel room and opened up the file on my laptop, but nothing jumped out at me.

CHAPTER NINE

The next night was dinner with Chris Badinovitch, my longtime friend from our football days at UCLA, and his wife, Jill. They had recently moved to a duplex off Doheny Drive at the south end of Beverly Hills. Chris, captain of detectives in Beverly Hills, had strong pressure to move there from Agoura Hills. There was a concerted push by the Beverly Hills PD to bring all their officers within the city limit. With the sale of their Agoura home, some savings, and a good mortgage they were able to buy the duplex, the rent from the lower half paying the bulk of their mortgage.

For the first time in a long time, I went by myself, as Juliette was working late that day. Jill and Chris were concerned that we had broken off our relationship, but I assured them that Juliette was indeed working, solving a last-minute costume emergency on her latest movie.

I decided to up my game from the usual Malbec, and drank a single malt whisky to my dinner with Chris and Jill, which all of us enjoyed. I had gone back and forth between a Laphroaig, Glenfiddich, and the nearby Balvenie, and finally settled on "The Balvenie Double Wood 12"

I prefer the Laphroaig, but Chris found it a

little too smoky. In honor of the housewarming, I also brought along a bottle of Dom Pérignon 2009, a present from a grateful client. This seemed the perfect occasion to recycle the gift. I hoped the champagne was still good, as I stored it following stringent instructions.

Their new duplex was east of Doheny Drive and south of Olympic Boulevard. Externally it was gorgeous with all the Spanish accents of curved tops of windows and doors. I was surprised at how large their upper half was, a full three bedrooms and three bathrooms of about 2,000 square feet. The garden went to the lower half of the duplex.

While giving me the tour, "We inherited this charming family," Jill explained to me, and they are more than happy that we also use the garden.

The dinner was Jills' favorite, grilled salmon with new potatoes and asparagus, washed down with copious amounts of wine. An apple tart with vanilla ice cream completed the meal.

After the meal, Chris and I moved to his study, which was the smallest of the three bedrooms. Apart from the usual desk and computer set up, there were a couple of well-worn leather armchairs facing a 60-inch television. We settled down with glasses of The Balvenie and a pair of cigars that looked suspiciously Cuban, but which Chris, with a wink, insisted were from Costa Rica.

After puffing our cigars and sipping our

whisky, Chris asked me 'the question.'

"So, what does your gut tell you?"

I expressed my frustration that so far I had not made any progress with the Josie Broadmoor drowning.

"I'm almost certain it has to do with the life vest, but no idea how."

"Did you bring the video from the kid?"

"His name is Brendan, and yes."

I gave him the USB stick which he connected to the big TV.

"Let's take a screen grab of all the times we can see the life vests."

The first screen grab was just as the boat appeared over the horizon. Thanks to Brendan's hi-res equipment we were able to zoom on it. We kept comparing that screen grab to subsequent views of the life vests.

"There," Chris said. He took another screen grab. "See how the vests are now in a different place."

Sure enough, one vest was moved from the third to the fourth peg.

We zoomed in to the maximum allowed by the equipment.

"See anything?" asked Chris.

"Not really."

"Hang on" and with that Chris pulled a magnifying glass from the desk drawer.

We looked closely and finally saw it. Compared to the other life vests, the one hanging on peg three, in addition to the horizontal seam, tiny vertical stitches suggested the life vest had been opened and closed with the extra stitches. The stitches were so fine and color-matched the orange of the life vest that they were practically invisible.

"How about them apples?" this from Chris.

"Yeah, that's a smoking gun for sure. What next?"

"You have to get hold of the life vest."

Driving home carefully, being aware that I had probably drunk more than I should have for safe driving, I thought about the next step. I texted Chip to see if he would be there at sunset the next day. He replied in the affirmative.

The next evening, I made my way back to the Marina. Chip was already at the gate.

"They're waiting for you. I told them you're on the way."

Sure enough, the Marshalls greeted me like a long-lost son, putting a large glass of chardonnay in my hand, and settling down to watch the sunset. Once the sun had faded below the horizon they asked what they could do for me.

"Could I take another look at the life vests?"

"No problem. Knock yourself out."

I examined them with high expectations, but was disappointed that there was no life vest with the extra stitching. I did notice the number 07/12 in small type on one of the vests, and upon closer examination of the remaining four vests saw that three of them also had the number 07/12, the fourth having the number 11/19. Twain confirmed that the Police had taken away the sixth life vest. I assumed the numbers were the dates of manufacture.

"Did you replace the life vests when you bought the boat?"

"Yes, standard practice," replied Twain, "we replaced all six."

As I was leaving, a thought occurred to me. "Did Michael ever take the boat out on his own?"

It was Polly who replied, "Once, about two to three months ago."

"Did he say why?"

"Something about his old University department checking some measurements on a student thesis. Darling, do you remember what Michael said?"

"Something about this student finding a strange anomaly between depth and temperature just beyond the Marina Boat Channel. There was a third thing."

"Salt," said Polly hesitantly.

"Salinity," I suggested.
"That was it. Temperature, depth, and salinity. He had all these instruments he was going to use."

With profuse goodbyes all around, I made my way off the boat, well-lubed with wine.

Even though I was disappointed that I did not find the smoking gun, the life vest with the extra stitches, I was nevertheless pleased to have discovered that one life vest had a different date suggesting that it was a replacement. It was a long shot, but I hoped that Brendan had a video showing the exchange.

CHAPTER TEN

First things first. I had to contact Brendan Hampstead to see if he had any files I had not seen. To that end, I called Edna Hampstead, who, with a warm greeting told me that Brendan was back from Tahoe and would be home around 5 p.m.

Why don't you come over at about four and we could have some wine and chat some more? I agreed with enthusiasm.

Before setting out for Mast Court in the Marina, I called Josie, sister of Joyce Hampstead.

"Hello Mr. Lester, any news for me?"

"Only circumstantial. I am nearly a hundred percent sure that the life vest your sister wore had been tampered with. I filled her in on the stitching and the anomaly of the date on one of the life vests."
"Wouldn't the police have noticed the life vest was different?"

"No. I suspect that Michael Broadmoor switched the life vests before the police boarded, hence the one with the stitching. The odd date suggests that he disposed of it with a new one identical to all the others on board. Almost certainly the one that the police have has the date 07/12. We need a lot of luck to find a smoking gun." I assured her I would keep her up to date.

I got to the house on Mast Court just after 4 p.m. We greeted each other like long-lost friends. Edna had a bottle of La Finca Malbec, one of my favorite low-cost red wines from Trader Joe's, set up on the table in the small garden of the house. You would think that for one million-plus you would at least get a sizable garden, but the builders figured that the nearby beach could be your garden. Once again we started talking about travels past when out of the blue Edna asked, "Do you like opera?"

"I'm not sure. My parents were big opera buffs and used to take me along when I was young, mainly to the lighter ones. They were always going to the LA Opera, and a couple of times a year would go to the Met in New York."

"Do they still go?"

"Not as much since they now live in Phoenix. Last year, they went to Germany to that place where they play the complete Wagner Ring Cycle."

"Bayreuth."

"Gesundheit."

"That's the place, not a sneeze."

"I know. I was just teasing you."

"I knew you were a bad one the moment I saw you." With that, we finished off our first glasses of wine.

"Why did you ask about the opera?"

"I have two tickets for next week, but my usual friend who goes with me can't go."
"What are they playing?"

"Verdi's Turandot."
"Isn't that the one with the nasty Princess?"

"If you mean the Princess who gives suitors for her hand in marriage three riddles to solve, and when they fail she has them beheaded, then yes, I believe that the description of 'nasty' applies."

"But one guy solves the riddles?"

"Yes, but if she guesses his name before sunrise, she can still have him beheaded."

"What a charmer."

"Let me put on an Aria. You'll probably recognize it immediately."

I instantly recognized Nessun Dorma, nobody sleeps, with the last lines, 'Vincero, Vincero, I will win, I will win.'

"You recognized it?"

"Of course. It's the one that Pavarotti used to sing at Italian soccer matches."

"So, you'll come?"

"Yes, on one condition, that you come with me to a jazz club I've been meaning to go to on Sunset Boulevard in Hollywood."

"Agreed" and with that, we settled down with our glasses of wine to hear the finishing bars of Turandot.

As the music faded into the Marina sky, Brendan came into the garden and kissed his aunt on the cheek.

"Hello Mr. Lester, nice bike. I thought you told me that you had an old Suzuki?"

"Hello Brendan, and yes I traded the old Suzuki for this low mileage one-owner Triumph Speed Triple."

"I would like a Ducati."

"Me too. I road-tested one, but it was too much bike for me."

"Do you want the strobe put on this one?"

"Yes but the car first." I fished two hundred dollars out of my pocket and gave it to him.

"Can you and your friend whose name I have forgotten?"

"Trevor."

"Yeah, Trevor. Anyway, can you do it next Wednesday evening when your aunt and I are going to the opera?"

"Sure, what are you going to?"

"Turandot. It's all about this princess beheading her suitors and putting their heads on poles outside her castle."

"Cool," and I think he meant it.

"Can you do the car here?"

"For sure. I'll need your cell phone number."

"I gave him my 310-area code number and the two hundred dollars.

"Brendan, there is one more thing. Do you have any more videos from the Marina?"

"Sorry, no," then added, "I do have GoPro files of me chasing sports cars from the parking lot. I got Lambos, Porches, Vettes, I even have the C8, and of course lots of Ferraris."

"What about a Bentley convertible?" thinking about Joyce's car.

"Too slow."

Brendan explained that he was referring to the GoPro Helmet Hero HD video camera, designed for sports.

At my request, he gave me a USB stick with all of them.

I left with goodbyes all around.

There were over a hundred GoPro files. In addition to sports cars, Brendan had mentioned there were a couple of Audi R10s and a McLaren P1. In many of the videos, Brendan started pedaling furiously after the car but lost it as soon as it turned onto Washington Boulevard and accelerated out of sight. It was only when there was heavy traffic that he had a chance of following them. I fast-forwarded through the files hoping for a miracle. There were eight red Ferraris. Unfortunately, Brendan did not start the files until the cars started moving, so there was no identification of any of the drivers. He lost the first two. The third made a left from Washington onto Pico, He managed to follow it to Santa Monica. When the driver got out it was not Michael Broadmoor. The next two red Ferraris were equally dead ends, but the sixth was a jackpot. The license was P888KVB7. There were no other Ferraris in the files. I was surprised as this license plate, ending with a seven, belonged to Tom Dickenssen and not Michael Broadmoor. Brendan kept up with it in the mid-afternoon traffic. He followed it up to Washington Boulevard, across Pico, and then as it made a right turn into a side street. The Ferrari stopped, and what appeared to be a box flew out of the passenger window right into a nearby dumpster with an open top. The car then sped away. Brendan went flat out for about one hundred yards, then gave up. As he turned around to go back to Washington Boulevard, his GoPro swept over the dumpster. I had to rewind a few times but finally realized that a figure had dashed into the frame, had looked inside the dumpster, had picked up the box thrown out of the Ferrari, and had run off with it. I managed a screen grab of the person who took it, thin, six feet tall, bald head, goatee mustache wearing a red parka, and tan slacks.

The fact that it was Tom Dickenssen's Ferrari, and not that of Michael Broadmoor, had me scolding myself for breaking one of my cardinal rules, 'don't go for the shiny object, and keep an open mind.'

This time, the 'shiny object' had been Michael Broadmoor. It was clear that I would have to do a deep dive into the Dickenssens. I called CT and asked him to do the usual 'possible suspect' review.

CHAPTER ELEVEN

I had invited Edna to dinner before the showing of Turandot. I had also arranged for a town car to take us from the restaurant to the opera house, and then home, but there was no point in paying for them to sit through our dinner, so we took an Uber to the nearby Sapori restaurant, Edna's choice. After the mixed appetizer, Edna had the fish of the day, and forsaking my usual spaghetti carbonara, had the New Zealand lamb. Even though Edna had fish, we washed it down with a bottle of Chianti Classico. We had a spirited conversation about our various travel adventures, and before we knew it, it was time to leave for the opera. The choice of a town car was both utilitarian and selfish, as I felt we would not be constrained in our alcohol consumption.

It had been many years since I had been to the opera. The last time had been with my parents was when I was about fifteen years old. I vaguely remembered that it had been La Boheme. This Turandot was fun.

At the interval, I managed to snag a couple of glasses of champagne, then checked my phone for messages. I had put my phone on silent, having read stories of conductors stopping their music in midflight when interrupted by a cell phone, allowing the entire audience to cast withering looks at the hapless perpetrator.

There were two messages, the first from Brendan.

"We have finished installing the strobe alarm. Instructions for downloading the phone app with your keys."

I showed the message to Edna.

"Such clever boys. Did you know Trevor designed the app himself?"

I didn't, but agreed that they were indeed very clever.

The second message was from CT, brief and to the point.

"Nothing on the Dickenssens yet, but I found your dumpster guy."

I had given CT the task of finding the dumpster thief. He was the perfect person for the job, because unlike me, CT had infinite amounts of patience and perseverance, and it appeared to have paid off.

I met him the next morning at the Culver City Starbucks.

"Man, this was some hunt," was his greeting to me.

When we collected our coffees from the bar he continued, "I hunted everywhere for this guy. I started in Venice, went on to Santa Monica, then the valley. I'm talking of three days of futile legwork."

"I then went into the Valley, and I finally got a break."
"That's BK, one of the guys in the San Fernando Mission told me."

"Do you know where he hangs out?"

"After some asking around he told me they all believed he was in the Long Beach Shelter."

"So, you found him?"

"Kinda. That was his home base, but he's gone by sun up, with no way to track him until he comes back, which sometimes is past midnight."

"I finally found him by going there at four in the morning. By the way, you owe me a good night's sleep."

"Anyway, as I was saying, I met him. His name is Robert Knightsbridge. Bob for short, hence the BK which he jokes is short for 'Black Knight.'"

"When I met him. I offered him breakfast, but he told me that the shelter had breakfast available, so we went off to the ubiquitous Starbucks."

"I asked him how he got there, as it was clear that he was not the usual homeless type."

"I was a high-flying IT guy, in charge of a new quantum computing startup that Google had partnered with. I was making around one point five mils, big house in Pacific Palisades, all the toys,

Ferraris, Lambos, Ducatis, speedboats, you name it, I had it."

"My wife is an ER doc. I was working over one hundred hours a week, and she was also working crazy hours. On one of the rare occasions when we were both at home at the same time, we just looked at each other."

"I can't do this anymore," I told her, "And with that, we agreed on a no-contest divorce. I gave her the house, all the toys, and half the brokerage account, more than enough to keep her in comfort for a long time."

"Did you change jobs?"

"In a way. I resigned from the startup and half-lived on the street until I ended up at the Long Beach Shelter. Now I look after all their IT needs. In return, I have my own cubicle, and meals when I need them."

"What do you do during the day?"

"When I lived in the Palisades, I was amazed by the stuff that people threw away in the dumpster, some of it brand new. Without a doubt could be very useful to someone who needed it."

"So that's what you do?"

"Yep. Every day I jump on the blue line downtown and then take one of the other rail lines to the valley, Pasadena, or wherever the mood takes me. Some days, I pick up one of the express buses to the end. My only requirement is that it's an affluent area."

"Can I take you back to a couple of weeks ago? You were off Washington Boulevard, north of Pico."

"Yeah, I remember that. I was about to look into a dumpster. I opened the top. When I noticed my shoelaces were loose. I bent down to tie them when I heard this sports car, a Ferrari."

"I knew what it was as I had a couple in my time. It came screeching to a stop and a box flew out of the passenger window, and off it went."

"You recovered the box?"

"Yeah, it was a life vest."

"BK, this is very important. What did you do with it?"

"I took it to the Goodwill on Venice Boulevard."

"I thanked him and offered him some money."

"Thanks, but no thanks. I have money but I limit myself to ten dollars a day."

And off he went.

"We have to get to the Goodwill right now."

We sped to the Goodwill on Venice Boulevard, and by a miracle found a parking space. We finally located the Manager and asked him about the life vest.

"We have hundreds of people coming in every day." He called over one of his volunteers.

"Paul, any chance you know who took that orange life vest?"

"Yeah, it was that Jap lady and her son."
"Japanese, Paul, Japanese."
"Sorry boss."

"OK. See if you can help the detectives track these people down?"

When I mentioned the word detective, I might have forgotten to add 'private.'

"She and her son come in almost most Saturdays, usually mid-morning."

"Thanks, Paul, see you tomorrow." Today being Friday.

CT and I got to Goodwill at ten a.m. I asked Paul to point out if he saw the Japanese lady and her son, but it was CT who saw her first. We got Paul to introduce us.

She's called Asahi Kobayashi, her son is Ted.

"Good morning Kobayashi-san" I greeted her, turning to her son I asked, *Nihongo hanasemasu ka?*"

"*Watashi ga yarimasu. Doko de sore o hanasu koto o manabimashita ka?*"

"I learned to speak it in the navy. I was based in Japan for a few years."

"Were you then a detective like NCIS?"

"Like that. But a little more underground."

Having done our language exchange, I asked him if he had taken the life vest.

"Yeah, it's really cool."

"Listen, Ted, this life vest is a really important item in a criminal investigation."

"How about a swap?" and with that, I showed him a fancy backpack that cyclists use. I had learned from Paul that Ted was always looking for items for his bicycle.

"Wow, for sure." As he took one look at the backpack.

"It's at our house we could go there now."

"Did you drive here?" "

"I wish, it takes us two buses."

"No problem. We'll give you a lift."

They had a small one-bedroom apartment on Pico Boulevard and 32nd street, right across the street from Trader Joe's. It was a third-floor walkup facing the street. The place was immaculate, and Mrs. Kobayashi insisted that we had some green tea before we made the swap. Not only was the life vest there, but Ted had kept the box.

"This is important Ted, did anyone else touch the life vest other than you?"

"No."

"Great. Could you give me something else with your fingerprints on it, for comparison and elimination purposes?"

He came back with a blank piece of shiny paper.

"I reckoned that the shiny paper would show up the fingerprints better."

He was right, and I thanked him for his help and smarts about the paper.

CHAPTER TWELVE

CT came by the office with his first pass at the Dickenssens. They ran a wholesale supply business, providing goods to businesses such as The Winslow Company owned By Joyce Broadmoor. As the company grew, it became, by far, Dickenssen's main client.

"I did some checking on them both, and surprise, surprise, Mr. Tom has quite a background. He had a lot of trouble as a juvenile, sealed but not forgotten. As an adult, he has a string of assaults with an array of weapons. A nasty piece of work our Mr. Dickenssen."

"He must have very good attorneys."

"Never did time inside?"

"Suspended, or at worst a few months home arrest."

"Then he must have really good attorneys. How about lately?"

"Nothing for at least ten years. There is a rumor that the company is in financial trouble, but as you know, that's not my thing."

I paid CT for all his extra time, plus a bonus for his successful tracking of the life vest then headed off to the office where Dolores, my longtime manager/assistant and invaluable helper, was waiting for me.

"So, you got it."

"Yes, including the shipping box," I told Dolores.

She picked up the box, wearing gloves, as I had done. "Amazon with the label ripped off."

"Isn't there another small barcode label on all their boxes?"

Dolores turned the box over and there it was.

'We have to find out whose box it was."

"Yeah, but it doesn't prove that whoever the box belonged to bought a new life vest, only that he bought something from Amazon."

"Dolores, we need that computer whiz nephew of yours."

"OK. But no questions asked, and the usual fee."

"Agreed. Have him track down the owner of the Amazon box. I also need a deep dive into the Dickenssens' company financial situation."

Dolores made a call and came back into my office.

"Piece of cake. Says he'll have all the info in two hours."

Less than two hours later, the wiz nephew

delivered as promised.

"Sorry, I could not get the Amazon info. Probably take me a while to break into their system, but I'm reluctant to do that."

"Tom Dickenssen is in deep doo-doo financially. The company's doing great. The problem is that they are owed a large amount by Winslow and he's not paying. Normally this would not be a problem as they use a factor to advance to them funds against receivable, but that only goes out for ninety days. Some of these bills are older than six months, and the factor wants his money. The rumor is that they might go belly up."

I got a hold of CT. "Can you find out why Winslow was not paying their supplier, Dickenssen?"

Well, this was a serious motive. But the question was, what were the Dickenssen doing on the boat with the Broadmoors?"

As the wiz nephew could not trace the Amazon box as yet, we needed plan B, which was to identify any fingerprints. For elimination, we had Ted's fingerprints, and CT had obtained those of BK, the dumpster guy, from a cup he had used at Starbucks. Tom Dickenssen's were in the system. With some foresight, I had got Michael Broadmoor's prints when last on the boat with the Marshalls.

I asked if there was anything that only Michael Broadmoor touched. It turned out that he was partial to a particular 'Ron Vicaro' Barbados rum. As the bottle was almost empty, they had no objection to my taking it away.

On the same trip, I asked them if anyone had touched any of the life vests since Joyce Broadmoor's drowning.

When they told me 'no,' I persuaded them to let me take the life vest with the date 11/19.

It took a full day until the lab I use came back to me with the fingerprint results. They were able to identify Ted and the dumpster guy, and there were several others. Among these was a print that also appeared on the rum bottle and the 11/19 vest. Unfortunately, there were several unknown prints on the 11/19 life vest.

It wasn't a large leap to the rum bottle and life vest prints to Michael Broadmoor. Normally I would have turned over the evidence to the police for the fingerprint analysis, but as there was no chain of custody for the Amazon box, I felt no guilt in having my lab do it.

There was still the problem of the Ferrari at the dumpster belonging to Tom Dickenssen. Here I kicked myself as it was so obvious, though I had some small excuse as it was dusk at the time of photography. I had gone downstairs and looked at license plates with ones and sevens and compared them with the screen grab of the license plate of the Ferrari at the dumpster. The seven was, without doubt, a doctored job, as the normal seven on the license plate slopped slightly to the left from top to bottom. The one on the license plate was a vertical stroke, indicating it was Michael Broadmoor's car, and he had added a small horizontal line at the top on the one, to throw off suspicion of himself and onto Tom Dickenssen.

Even though it was now moot, I got the story of the disagreement between the Dickenssens and Braodmoors from Polly Marshall.

"It was very silly. Mary Dickenssen had remarked that Michael Broadmoor was a bit of a leach on Joyce. Even though it was mainly true, Joyce Broadmoor got deeply offended, hence the split in the relationship. The boat trip together was an attempt to mend fences."

Dolores jolted me back to the main problem.

"We have to get into Michael Broadmoor's Amazon account."

"We have his email account, at least his business one."

"Unlikely he would use that one. We need his personal email."

"How?"

"From his secretary. You're going to have to do 'the I'm getting fired routine.' I'll call to make sure he's not in his office, then you're on."

Dolores put the call through to the

Winslow Building Company and asked for Michael Broadmoor's personal assistant.

"Kaillee Pasternak, how may I help you?"

"Are you Mr. Broadmoor's assistant?"

"Executive assistant" came back a rather stiff answer.

"Sorry, please help me. I'm Monica, working for Pacific Shores Investment Company and am sure Mr. Langley, the owner, will fire me."

"Excuse me, what?"

"Oh, please help me. I've only been back at work for a few weeks now that my son is in high school. I know he's going to fire me."

"How can I help?"

"Oh, it's so stupid. Mr. Langley is doing a special project for Mr. Broadmoor and asked me to send the information to his personal, not his work email account. He gave it to me, but I accidentally shredded it with a pile of documents."

"Oh, please help me, I remember it was something to do with chemistry."

"Was it "the alchemist'?"

"Yes, yes, that sounds right, is it Gmail?"

"No Suremail."
"Thank you, thank you, thank you, you've been a lifesaver."

"Happy to help."

With that Dolores turned to me with a look of satisfaction

thealchemist@suremail.com

"Now all you have to do is to solve his password."
"Piece of cake."

I believed her, for she had a genius-level feel for passwords.

I told Dolores that I needed to do a run and headed off to the Hollywood reservoir to do my usual 'huff and puff' taking the Beemer having had a bad experience with my motorcycle being punted into the woods below when some big SUV wanted my parking space. I remember that day well. I had been working on a case involving a stolen deposit from a Beverly Hills AI clinic. I had come to the reservoir on my motorcycle and parked it in the center of an available space. When I returned the bike was nowhere to be seen and had been pushed down the slope by someone aggrieved that a motorcycle would take up a parking space and had pushed over the edge of the downslope at the far end of the parking space. It had been a real pig to retrieve it.

During the run, everything on Broadmoor clicked into place, and it was clear to me what was missing to solve the case.

When I got back to the office, Dolores was

sitting there with a large smile of self-satisfaction.

"You solved it?"

"Yep. The thing about geniuses is that they can be predictable outside that area. Between the email "the alchemist" and his Toyota license plate "pbn2au" I felt it had to be in there somewhere and tried the license plate written out as "leadintogold" and it worked."

"Here is the printout of the life vest purchase. OK if I take the rest of the afternoon off?"

"No problem. I have to pick up Juliette from LAX."
"Give her my best."

Juliette was my 'on again off again' girlfriend and was now definitely 'on.' She was a freelance costume designer and was working in Paris on a series of movies from cavemen to modern times. She was back for a few days as a local film studio was trying to poach her for an upcoming movie.

Juliette Marianne McKintosh, her full name, had been born of a French mother and a Scottish father. Her parents had met in London where her future father was a graduate student in aeronautical engineering. Her parents moved to Montreal when her father got hired by Bombardier Aviation. A couple of years later, he was poached by Hughes aircraft, which is how they arrived in Los Angeles. A year after they arrived Juliette was born, and from a very early age, showed she was an art prodigy. Her parents nurtured her art gift, but insisted that she had a normal childhood and did not push her into attending college early. At eighteen, she moved to the Art Institute Chicago where she excelled.

In her junior year, she saw a notice from a local high school to help with costume design for an upcoming play. For a lark, she applied and got the 'gig.'

She had so much fun making what was a widely acclaimed set of costumes, she decided on a course change. In her final year, she took any class that had ~~any~~ relevance to costume design.

She attended FIDM in Los Angeles but left after a year, as the emphasis was too much on business and not design.

She saw an announcement in a trade magazine for a costume designer in a low-budget Sci-Fi movie, and as they say,' the rest is history.'

I had gone to LAX to meet her. She was one of the first off the plane and looked as spectacular as always. My height, slim as a reed, with classical French good looks. She was wearing skinny blue jeans with legs so long it almost looked as if she was on stilts. The jeans were paired with a pale blue cashmere sweater that perfectly matched the color of her eyes. She had cut her hair a little shorter and wore it into a French bob. To say she turned heads was an understatement.

I had asked her how she managed on film

locations because she was eclipsing the stars in looks.

"I let my hair fall where it wants, wear no makeup, and wear frumpy clothes. That seems to work, but mostly I'm not on the set, so my looks don't matter.

They greeted each other with a big hug.

"Ugh, flying business class, I may as well fly in the plane toilet."

I had to laugh, "Since when did you become such a snob?"

"Since everyone wants to hire me, and flies me first class."

"How long are you here for?"

"Only overnight. I'm seeing the studio tomorrow morning and flying back in the evening."

"I thought you were already working on a couple of movies in Paris?"

"I am. I have a workshop with half a dozen people working around the clock."

"But this project is here?"

"Frankly, I don't want to do it, but it's the same group that gave me my big break with the ZILL Sci-Fi low-budget movie, which was my first movie costume job. They're doing a sequel and really want me."

"Wasn't that based on a book?"

"Yes, ZILL by Gerald Ems. I very much enjoyed the book. It had so much meat for costume design."

She did not mention that she had been nominated for an Oscar for her costumes in her first Sci-Fi movie.

"It just came to me that we met at the wrap party for that film."

"My lucky day."

"I never asked you, how come you were there?"

"It may sound like a cliché, but I found the Director's lost dog."

She just laughed and said with a straight face, "That sounds like a shaggy dog story" and started laughing again.

"How would you manage to do the Paris movies and this one?"

"I already talked to Marjorie who helped me work on the first Sci-Fi movie, and we agreed to make it work. With available technology, we can move designs from Paris to here with no problems and can even do virtual fittings by computer. I would come back here every two or three weeks."

"Listen, chéri, I am so busy we never see each other. Why don't you come to Paris for a few weeks?"

"I'll give it my best shot. What time shall I pick you up for dinner?"

"Let's make it around 8 p.m. I'm going to take a

siesta."

I dropped her at the Hollywood Roosevelt Hotel, reminding her "8 p.m."

I struggled with myself whether to update Detective Sharrow on the case. Normally it was a no-brainer to update whichever police force was in charge of the case, but Sharrow had been so rude and dismissive the last time we met that it gave me pause. Finally, I realized that my wounded ego was getting the better of my common sense.

I drove over to the Marina PD, to meet with Detective Nathan Sharrow. Dolores had set up the meeting.

"I had to twist his arm. He felt you were a complete waste of time. Only when I told him that you had some real evidence did he reluctantly agree to ten minutes."

I arrived on time but had to wait almost an hour in a drafty corridor. No doubt this was to show me my insignificance. At our last meeting, his purple suit, fluorescent green shirt, and blue and yellow striped shirt were so color dissonant that I concluded that he had to be color blind.

"Your assistant said that you had some real evidence to show me," this said with a sarcastic eye roll.

I pulled the enlarged photos of the life vests when the Marshall's boat first appeared on the horizon, and then at the dock.

"You will notice that the life vests are not at the same locations in the two photos."

"Nothing unusual about that. People just put them back wherever there is a space."

"Hear me out. In the second photo, you can see stitching where the life vest in the new location has been tampered with by very fine stitching."

He looked at the photos for a long time, and then an amazing transformation took place. Detective Sharrow went from a bored, reluctant participant to fully engaged.

"I owe you an apology Mr. Lester. I thought you were nothing more than a jumped-up dog catcher."

"No apology necessary. I thought you were a jumped-up little prick."

With that mutual admiration out of the way we continued. I showed him the photo where the tampered life vest had been replaced. The Marshalls had never touched the life vest since the accident. Wearing gloves I put it in a plastic bag, then a storage locker.

I pulled my phone out, and then showed the video footage of Michael Broadmoor throwing the box, presumably containing the doctored life vest, into the dumpster.

Detective Sharrow's eyes widened at seeing the

video. "How did you get that?"

"Good detective work," at which he gave me a small nod of approval.

I put on some gloves, unzipped the sports bag I had brought with me, and with a flourish put the box from the dumpster on the table between us.

Nathan's eyes got wide. "Is that what I think it is?"

"Sure is. The fingerprints should be interesting."

He was all business. "I'll get a rush on it."

I pointed out that the box was from Amazon. "Can you get a subpoena to find what was in it?" not telling him that Dolores had broken into the account and that we had a printout of the life vest that Michael Broadmoor had bought.

We discussed the case some more.

"This is great circumstantial evidence. It would be nice if we could have some evidence tying Mr. Broadmoor to the tampering."

I agreed and told him I had a couple of ideas on the subject.

CHAPTER THIRTEEN

After an early breakfast at Juliette's hotel, I ran her over to the Palladium Studios on Pico Boulevard. It was an early start for a studio meeting, but Juliette had an early afternoon flight to Paris. We agreed I would pick her up at noon to take her to the airport.

I made my way down from Pico to Santa Monica to have a second breakfast with CT and Issy. They were at a distant corner table when I arrived. Today CT had Mini mouse as his cartoon figure T-shirt.

After they ordered full English breakfasts and I settled for a cup of coffee. I filled them in on all the evidence we had on Michael Broadmoor so far.

CT who had been involved in most of the case said, "Lots of circumstantial. We need a smoking gun."

Issy added, "He must have done some experiments somewhere."
"Exactly what I thought, but where?"

"I did some work on that, tasking Jimmy to do some snooping for me."

"I used 'Jimmy' whom you both know spent some time inside for hacking GPS in cars. As a former prisoner, he has difficulty finding steady work, but now works as a 'consultant' in GPS tracing."

He got back to me saying that Michael Broadmoor's Ferrari was a time before they installed GPS. Here is his message.

"Hello John, sorry no GPS available. On a hunch, I had a look at the major Insurance Companies to see if he had a safe driver driving app. He does but I need the ID, probably his email, and password."

"On a long shot, I sent him the information that Dolores had used to get into the Amazon account."

"Thanks, John, that worked. The app does not give addresses, only town locations. I looked at dates before and after the period you gave me"

I paused the message to tell CT and Issy that I had given Jimmy the date of the homicide.

I continued the message. "Before the date you gave, he went several times a week from the Marina to the City of Industry. No journeys after that."

"It makes sense," said Issy. "He didn't want the risk of being followed if he was under suspicion."

"Don't you find it strange that he has a safe driving app on his Ferrari?"

"Not really, I have one on the Beemer. It measures speed, acceleration braking, and cornering. It dings you with events if you do anything wrong. I usually have no dings, the most ever were two dings on one trip."

"Jimmy said that our Mr. Broadmoor often had more than ten per trip."

"Not surprising if you see how he was driving on Brendan's GoPro video. Man, he peeled out of the Marina parking lot. If he hadn't been caught in traffic on Washington Boulevard, Brendan could never have caught up to him on his bike."

"Back to my original question, how to find the location? The City of Industry has hundreds of industrial buildings."

"He's probably using a place that belongs to a friend. No ownership or rental trace."
"Good point, though it could be a rental."

"Issy, could you check out possible lab rental space in the City of Industry?"

I got Jimmy on the phone. "Jimmy, can you do a little phone hack?"

"No problem."

"I need a list of contacts on Michael Broadmoor's phone."

"Consider it done."

CT chimed in, "How about friends from his college days?"

"Best idea yet," I replied. "I'll check it out. Before that, let's meet again in a couple of days to see if we turned up anything locally."

It turned out that I had the answers later that day. Issy got back to me by phone.

"Seems like it's only a small number of brokers who handle lab space, and they all work together. I got talking to one of them, Mike Bramberg."

"This Bramberg guy told me that only three locations have been hired in the last year. He was a nice guy and showed me all three. Two were empty and the third was a stinko place that was extracting juice from rotten fruit. Don't ask me why."

It was unfortunate that the City of Industry was a bust. It could be that Michael Broadmoor had used lab space from someone he knew. Perhaps Jimmy would have more luck.

A short while after I hung up with Issy, Jimmy got me on the cell phone.

"I have somewhat good news and bad news."

"The 'somewhat' good news?"

"I managed to access a limited part of the phone. He has a 'friends' file. Unfortunately, they are only first names, and he has encryption on the phone numbers."

"You did fine, Jimmy, cash as always?"

"Please."

"I'll get it to you today. Text me the friend list."

A few minutes later the list arrived.

"Sammy, Ike, Wambo, Roger Simon, and JJ."

Time for a road trip.

I called The College of Chemistry at UC Berkeley and asked who might have been there some twenty years ago.

"That would be Clara Williamson. She's been here forever. There's a rumor that she moved in as they were putting up the building."

"Can I set up an appointment with her?"

"She only comes in a couple of times a week. Would next Tuesday work for you?"

I was disappointed that it was not sooner but agreed to 10 a.m.

"Is there a hotel nearby?"

"The Graduate Berkeley hotel is close. It's an easy walk to us."

The next Tuesday at about 9.30 am I called and asked for Clara Williamson.

"This is Clara Williamson."
"Good morning Mrs. Williamson, this is John Lester, your ten o'clock."

"Good morning, what can I do for you?"

"I'm going over to Café Strada to get a coffee before our meeting. Can I bring you anything?"

"That is most kind. I would love a Caramel Frappuccino."

"Whipped cream?"

"Please."

"See you at ten."

Clara Williamson was a small lady dwarfed by the desk in front of her. Silver hair as befitted her age with a pair of horn-rimmed glasses hanging around her neck by a silver chain. She was dressed in what looked like a hand-knitted dark brown sweater and blue jeans. I had expected a costume from the Victorian period from the way the department secretary had described her.

She greeted me warmly. "I thank you for the coffee. In all the years that I have had meetings, you are the first to offer and bring me coffee."

"It's in the form of a bribe," I told her. "That's a very nice sweater, handmade?"

She preened a little. "By my own hand. Yes, your 'bribe' worked. So, what can I help you with?"

"It's about a Dr. Michael Broadmoor who graduated some twenty years ago." I decided to give him his full title, as not only did he earn his doctorate, but surely that is how he would have been known by Berkeley.

"I vaguely remember him. Brilliant student, but very full of himself."

I decided that I would be straightforward with her and explained that I was investigating a homicide in which he was a suspect.

"That would not completely surprise me. He was extremely self-centered, and always insisted on having his way."

"Would you remember any of his friends?"

"Boy, that was a long long time ago."

"How about I try some first names on you?"

"Go for it."

I started to go through the list that Jimmy had sent me. When I got to Ike, she held up her hand to stop me.

"Ike strikes a bell." She rocked back and forward in her chair, eyes closed.

"Ike Winter something. Let me look at our doctorate index."

"It's online if you know where to look. Here it is, Dr. Ike Winterberg."

"Any chance you could find out where he is right now?"

"It would be in the alumni information, but that is confidential, and you would need a password."

"Surely after your long service with the department, you would have obtained the password."

She gave me an impish grin, "You could always bribe me with another coffee."

"Done, but even better how about an early lunch?"

After a light lunch at a local Chinese restaurant of her choosing, I got on the I5 back to LA with the address of Dr. Ike Winterberg in Pacific Palisades.

CHAPTER FOURTEEN

I met with CT and Issy at the Starbucks in Culver City. We managed to grab a table away from the crowd. I brought them up to date on my visit to Berkeley.

"I met with this very nice and helpful lady. She told me that Michael Broadmoor only had one friend, a Dr. Ike Winterberg."

To quote her, "Drs. Winterberg and Broadmoor were both self-centered egoists at the center of their mutual self-admiration."

She went on to say, "It was surprising that they became friends, as in 'like magnets usually repel like.' I think they saw themselves in the other person. For sure neither had any other friend within the department."

"Ok guys, if it's anyone it's this Winterberg guy."

"As I see it we have four possible avenues:

1) Ask Winterberg if Michael Broadmoor used lab space. You know the first thing that will happen is that he will call Broadmoor.

2) Hack the GPS on his car. According to Clara Williamson at Berkeley, the only redeeming thing about our Dr. Winterberg is that he loved

classic cars. He was a wiz at repairing them, both his and other people's. It's likely that's what he drives, so no GPS.

3) Look into his real estate ownership in the City of Industry. I suspect any ownership would be under a company name and not his own. Just in case CT, can you run a check on that?

4) We tail him from his Pacific Palisades home. Tedious, but I believe our best shot."

While I was outlining our options, CT brought up Ike Winterberg's house on Google Street View. It was a street with enormous houses. There were a few delivery trucks and a couple of pickups that had gardening equipment in the back. It was clear that anyone parked on the street, which we would need to do, would stand out and immediately be flagged by local security.

We all said in unison, "Too many roads out, and nowhere to hide."

Issy said the obvious conclusion. "We would need a team of at least three to cover the exits. It would be much better to put a tracker on his car."

CT volunteered to do that this very night. The challenge was to get to the car which was surely parked in the garage. Using a special multi-band garage door opener was the easiest solution, but the noise of the garage door opening would alert anyone in the house. In looking at the street view there was a side door to the garage which probably could be broken into.

"It might take me a couple of visits to solve the door."

"What about security devices?" asked Issy.

"Once I get the door open it should take me less than a minute to place the tracker. I'll close the door. When they investigate, they'll think it was a faulty sensor or the wind."

"I have another idea."

CT asked, "What if someone asked what we are doing here?"

"Print up business cards showing that you are selling zero-scaping."

It was three days before my idea worked.

It was Issy who called. "The tracker is installed."

"It went as you suggested. The car was still in the driveway ready to go out. We stopped and admired the car. A gardener came over."

"Hola."

"Hola, bonito coche," CT replied.

"Si bonito coche, sin embargo por favor tenga cuidado, el dueño se vuelve loco si alguien toca el coche."

"No problema."

"We drove off. I asked Issy if he had installed

the tracker."

"Piece of cake. What did he say?"

"Just that the owner goes crazy if anyone touches his car."

"Good job, you two. Now we can see where he goes."

It took three days, but finally Dr. Ike Winterberg led us to his lab in the City of Industry. It was a large warehouse-type building with a list of tenants listed on the outside. One of the listings was Chemical Pollution Testing Co.

"Let's see if he goes out for lunch," I told CT who was with me.

Sure enough, on the stroke of twelve, he roared off in his classic car.

We walked through the front door that accessed all the businesses and followed the signs for the lab that took us to the far left-hand corner.

Just inside the entrance to the lab was a young lady in the ubiquitous white lab coat with the name of the company stitched on with the name Trina below it.

"Good morning, I'm afraid that you just missed Dr. Winterberg."

"That's OK, we were just passing by on the way to a client and saw your sign. I'm James Ironson environmental detective, showing her my card, which I had printed up that morning."

"Do you have a catalog?"

Trina handed one to me.

"I never met an environmental detective before."

"It's a new profession. Can you show us around?"

"I can give you a quick tour. We have the latest high-resolution testing equipment. We have the usual gas chromatograms, HPLC, Mass spectrometers, FTIR atomic absorptions, and so on. Our instruments are so sensitive that there is no such thing as 'below detection.' We are particularly proud of our air sampling containers. They are designed to only open under vacuum to prevent contamination."

I had noticed a small room with a door with the sign, Dr. Michael Broadmoor. Through the glass panel on the door could be seen outside windows.

"I know it's a cheeky question, but how many people work in there?"

"Normally, Dr. Winterberg and a couple of lab techs."

"I noticed a sign for a Dr. Broadmoor. Does he also do pollution type of testing?"

"I don't believe so. He doesn't interact with Dr.

Winterberg's lab, but they do have lunch together when they are both here."

"Is he here often?"

She gave me a 'why are you asking look,' but replied, "usually once or twice a week unless the boys are out of school."

"They like working with their dad?"

"They seem to, though they occasionally come in without him. They're nice kids, leastwise the older one is, though the younger one is weird."

"In what way?"

"It's hard to put a finger on it. The best thing that I can describe is that he's completely lacking in social skills. Doesn't look you in the eye, no greetings or handshakes. Stuff like that."

Typical signs of juvenile autism I thought to myself.

We made our thanks, left the building, and walked around the back to where we estimated Dr. Broadmoor's lab would be.

Just as we peered into the window, my cell phone rang. It was detective Sharrow. After our last mutual admiration meeting, we had exchanged cell phone numbers.

"Detective Sharrow here, Mr. Lester," he said redundantly as his number had come up on my screen.

"Good morning detective, any news?"

"We followed up on the leads you gave us with success. The number from the Amazon box corresponds to a purchase of a life vest identical to the new one on the Marshall's boat."

"Excellent."

"As you suspected, Dr. Broadmoor's fingerprints were on that life vest, but none for the Marshalls, which is unusual considering that they have had their boat for several years."

"I'm glad that my theory proved out."

"Anyway, to show you that we really can do detective work ourselves, we tracked the thread used on the life vest. We traced it to a surgical supply house."

"Strange."

"Yes, but I'll come back to that. Nobody at the supply house recognized the thread until they brought in this older guy from the back. He recognized it immediately."

"That's our 2971B thread."
"Do you still carry it?"

"Oh yes. It used to be very popular until self-dissolving stitches came in."

"Can you check any sales in the last few months?"

"It turned out there was only one sale some

three months ago. I asked them about cameras."

"Yes, sorry but they overwrite after each week. That's when the young guy broke in. "I remember the IT guy saying something about it being saved to a cloud thingy. I got his number from them, and I'm waiting for him to get back to me."

"It seems a strange choice of thread."

"I agree, but I believe that he went on the internet and was only interested in the color match, nothing else."

"Mr. Lester, anything new from you?"

I told him about my trip to Berkeley.

"We followed Dr. Winterberg to a street in City of Industry. We'll probably find the location of the lab soon."

I didn't tell him about hacking Dr. Broadmoor's safe and drive app or putting a tracker on Dr. Winterberg's car.

We looked into the lab from the outside. There was a whole shelf of what appeared to be various salts as well as all types of measuring and mixing equipment.

In the far corner was a steel cupboard with a combination lock.

"Looks easy to open with a stethoscope," said CT

"Do you have one?" I asked him.

"Does a duck quack?" was his reply.

"Did anyone see any security sensors?"

"No," was the simultaneous reply.

Two nights later found us outside the main door. It wasn't even locked; not a very secure arrangement as it provided access to all the businesses in the building.

Entry into the Chemical Pollution Testing Co was easy, just a quick slide of a card. The door to Dr. Broadmoor's lab proved just as easy. Once inside, the view was exactly as from the outside. It looked like any other lab.

CT got to work on the combination lock. It took him all of a minute to open it.

Inside the cupboard, the world was much more interesting. There were three large notebooks, labeled "Dissolution experiments," "Gas production experiments," and "Swimming pool experiments."

I photographed the first few pages of each notebook.

In addition, in a locked cupboard there was 'the smoking gun' in the form of several life vests, each with a zipper to allow access to the inside of the life vest.

"Wow, jackpot," and similar expressions were said by all of us.

"We have to have a carrot to induce the police to get a search warrant for this place," I said. "I don't think his name on the lab door will be enough," showing them a photo I had surreptitiously taken of the nameplate on the door.

"We could leave a notebook in plain view on one of the benches."

"Too obvious. Michael Broadmoor could easily claim entrapment."

It was Issy who suggested hiding a life vest under a bench with a part of it just showing.

"It could look as if it had been out of sight, so he forgot to hide it."

As it had been Issy's idea, he got to hide the life vest.

I sent CT outside to make sure that the positioning was exact, then take a photo from outside and text me.

Issy and I looked at the photo and agreed it was perfect.

I decided to call Josie Pedersen. By now we were on a Josie and John name basis.

"Hello John, do you have news for me?"

"I do indeed. I believe that we are very close to cracking the case wide open. There is a one hundred percent chance that Michael Broadmoor tampered with the life vest." I then brought her up to date on all the evidence we had, plus that obtained by the police.

My next call was to Nathan Sharrow on his cell phone.

"Ah, good morning to my favorite dog catcher."

"Well hello to you, detective extraordinaire. I'm sending you a photo of what we believe is the lab. As you can see in the photo, there appears to be a piece of a life vest hidden under the far workbench."

"Great. I also have news. The IT guy from the supply house came through. Unfortunately, it wasn't Michael Broadmoor who bought the thread, but a young kid wearing dark glasses and a cap. As he came out of the store, a big gust of wind blew off his cap and we have a perfect shot of him. I've no idea who it is."

"Long shot. Do you have a photo of his kids?"

"Do not."

"Get one. I suspect Broadmoor used one of his sons as a pickup messenger."

"Will do."

CHAPTER FIFTEEN

There was no doubt that the police would have Broadmoor in for questioning. Detective Sharrow and I discussed timing.

"I don't think it's a good idea to search the lab. Ike Winterberg would call him immediately, and he would be gone."

I also said to Sharrow that Josie Pedersen told me that the stores had been sold for one hundred and twenty million dollars, which meant that Michael Broadmoor had at least eighty million at his disposal.

"Michael was negotiating with a couple of national chains. He was willing to take a discount for a quick sale. Offers were slow, when out of the blue, this French company, a subsidiary of the supermarket chain Carrefour, offered full price with a seven-day closing. He jumped at it like a trout after a juicy fly."

"That is a lot of fleeing money," agreed Detective Sharrow, and decided, "we will hold off the search until we have him in our custody."

As I rang off with the detective, I got a text from Juliette. "Coming back to LA Thursday to finalize costume deal. How about a weekend in the wine country?"

I replied with a whole line of smiling emojis.

"I'll meet your flight."

"AF 66 arriving 13.10."

I got a surprising message from Detective Sharrow. "We are interviewing Dr. Michael Broadmoor at 10 am tomorrow. Since you provided all the initial clues, we are inviting you to observe the interview."

I replied with an enthusiastic affirmation.

I got to the Marina police station at 9.45 a.m. and was met by Nathan Sharrow who took me to the observation area of the interview room. Already there was his boss, John Winston, head of detectives, and Andrea Snodgras from the district attorney's office, who when being introduced, said pointedly right at me, "I want to make sure that all evidence was obtained legally. This is a clever guy, and I don't want to give him a chance to get away because we did not follow the law."

I'm happy to say that I didn't even blink when she said that. Luckily, she could not read my mind, which was reviewing all the shortcuts we had done.

I noticed that Sharrow was dressed conservatively, everything well color coordinated. John Winston must have noticed my reaction. He whispered in my ear, "He has a new girlfriend with good fashion and color sense."

I nodded my agreement.

Michael Broadmoor was brought into the room by a couple of uniforms. He was dressed in what could be charitably said was Florida golf dress, clearly expensive, the blue sweater too blue, the plus-fours too stripy, the socks too yellow, and so on. He sat there with a superior smirk on his face as he was read his Miranda rights, clearly believing that he was by far the smartest person in the room. He was told that he was being charged on suspicion of the murder of his wife Josie Broadmoor. The police slow-walked the fingerprinting and photography to allow more time for the team that had gone to search the lab.

Nathan was joined in the interview room by a tech who made sure that all video and audio equipment was working properly.

The interview started with the usual routine questions of identification, domicile, etc. Nathan pulled out the photos of the change of life vests as the boat came into the harbor, pointing out the extra line of thread.

Michael Broadmoor looked surprised and then just sniffed, "A different thread on a life vest doesn't prove anything."

"What if we could show your son buying that thread?" He then showed him the photo of his son in the supply store.

Broadmoor took a look, smirked, and said, "that could be anyone."

"How about this photo showing your younger son after his cap was blown off?"

"He has many hobbies, so this is probably for one of them," said with just a shade less confidence.

Detective Sharrow repeated his question, asking Dr. Broadmoor if he wanted his attorney present.

Dr. Broadmoor again declined and seemed to sneer at the idea that he needed one. Nathan looked at the tech to make sure that the answer had been recorded.

"By the way, your son was the first person in 'ages,' their words, to buy this particular thread."

"So, what, it's just a thread."

"May we offer you water, coffee, or juice?"

"Water would be appreciated."

With a "be right back," Nathan left the room. All recording was paused.

It was a good ten minutes before he came back with a bottle of water and a plastic cup. He was buying a bit more time for the lab search.

After Michael Broadmoor had taken a drink of water, the recorders were turned back on.

"Let me show you this." Nathan passed over a

photo showing Broadmoor throwing a box out of his car into the dumpster.

This one took Michael Broadmoor by surprise, and there was an instantaneous look of doubt before his smirk returned.

"No law against throwing a box into the dumpster."

"Then have a look at this." It was a blowup of the bar code on the Amazon box.

"As you can see, the Amazon bar code is clear. Even though the address label had been torn off the box, the bar code was enough for Amazon to track the package to you, and the contents of the box to be a life vest."

A little more doubt crept into his eyes.

"Oh yes, I forgot to add that the manufacturing date of the life vest bought from Amazon matched the one on the boat."

"Coincidence. People are always replacing life vests."

"Very true. But what is interesting is that this life vest, which we found on the Marshall's boat had your fingerprints on it, but none from the Marshalls."

"Don't you think it strange that all other life vests on the boat were smothered with the Marshall's fingerprint, but this one had none?"

Michael Broadmoor had no answer to this.

There was a knock at the door. A hand beckoned Detective Sharrow.

"Why don't we take a break? This may be a few minutes. Can we get you anything while you wait?"

"A latte would be nice."
"We'll send one of our people to the Starbucks up the street."

"In that case, how about a lemon slice to go with it?"

"You've got it."

Detective Sharrow came into the observation room and invited us all to a table where the evidence from Dr. Broadmoor's lab had been laid out.

His first question to the detectives present was, "Were all the chain of evidence protocols followed, and was the evidence properly logged?"

Upon being assured that all procedures had been correctly followed, he put on gloves and looked through three notebooks that had been in the safe.

"We didn't see these when we looked in through the window."

Nathan turned to me, "They were in the cupboard with the combination lock."

"You opened that quickly."

"It was easy. One of my guys told me that the combination had been pasted on the underside of one of the desk drawers."

I had to smile to myself as I recalled CT's comment as he pasted the paper with the combination in place.

"This will never work."

Issy had bet him ten dollars that it would, and indeed it did.

Nathan put all the evidence into a large leather bag.

He returned to the interview room with the tech and the rest of us into the observation room.

Michael Broadmoor thanked him for the coffee and lemon slice.

"We are back on the record. Dr. Broadmoor, we found your lab."

"How do you know it was my lab?"

"Well, how do we know that, let me see, oh yes, your name was on the door."

Nathan could not help showing a small smile of satisfaction.

Once again he made the offer of Michael Broadmoor's attorney being present.

The guy who thought he was so much cleverer

than anybody else, again declined the offer.

"We found these," pulling out several life vests onto the table.

"More interesting are these notebooks. We only had a quick look, but we found the swimming pool experiments most interesting."

You could see Michael Broadmoor's demeanor completely change.

"You've got me." He admitted.

"Why don't you tell us the whole thing? Surely you don't want to be tried by twelve people of average intelligence."

"Yeah, Ok."

Nathan made the attorney offer again.

"Nah, that ship has sailed."

Broadmoor started to explain.

"It was a very challenging physics and chemistry problem."

There was not a flicker of compassion in his voice. He continued as if lecturing to a college class.

"I started by testing various salts, but that was far too slow. The problem is that when you take the material out of the life vest, the covering is cloth, so you have to stuff the vest completely full to maintain the shape."

"I then tried foaming salts like sodium bicarbonate. You know the stuff in Alka Seltzer."

"So how to dissolve the interior of the life vest quickly while maintaining the shape? The answer was foam. I found a loose foam that dissolved quickly in water. To make it more effective I remove the stitching from one of the upper panels of the life vest and held it in place with a small amount of water-soluble glue."

Everyone in both the interview and observation rooms were completely silent as Michael Broadmoor paced back and forth as he continued to lecture.

"I did time dissolution tests in the lab comparing ocean temperature and salinity to that of my swimming pool. There was just over a two-fold time difference."

"The swimming pool test had the life vest filling up with water in about one minute and fifteen seconds, which corresponded to just under three minutes in the ocean. I reasoned that when she fell off the back of the boat it would take at least that long to turn the boat around to look for her."

I thought to myself, 'she,' not Josie, not my wife, just 'she.' It only was a science experiment to him.

"Of course, that was only half the problem. I had to re-inflate the life vest to bring it back to the surface."

Again 'it', and not Josie or my wife.

"I solved that with some high-density foam under pressure in a canister inside the life vest. I had to hold the top in place with a clasp that was, in turn, held in place with water-soluble glue, enough that it took about three minutes to dissolve."

"When the foam escaped from the canister it filled the whole life vest and drove the air out of the loosened top flap. Back on the surface, the life vest looked perfectly normal."

"Unfortunately, some of the foam also escaped out of the flap onto the surface of the life vest. That was a challenging problem."

"I solved that with the use of magnets that were weak enough to let the flap open to let the air out, but strong enough to hold under foam inflation. Unfortunately, even the weakest magnets were too strong to let the air out. I solved that by cutting down the magnets until they worked as I wanted." He looked very pleased with himself as he explained the magnet solution.

"You tested all of these various trials in the swimming pool?"

He hesitated before saying, "Yeah. I couldn't use air tanks as that would have changed the parameters of the experiment. I just used a simple breathing tube. The final iteration worked perfectly, sinking in one minute twenty seconds, and re-inflating in three minutes."

Again, he looked tremendously pleased with himself.

There was a long silence while everybody digested all this information.

Finally, Nathan Sharrow broke the silence, "You switched the life vests once your wife was back on deck."

Yes, I threw it over to the area of the life vests. It was wet enough that when no one was looking I swapped positions for one hanging on one of the pegs. It continued to drip on the one below so that when the police wanted the life vest, I pointed to the one on the deck. They did not notice that the one on the peg above was also wet."

"You then arranged to buy a replacement life vest and do a swap with the doctored vest when no one was looking."

"Yes. I never suspected that someone would see me doing it."

Again Nathan, "Why did you do it?"

"I was tired of being a pauper, and always being second fiddle."

If being a pauper meant a house on The Venice Canals and a Ferrari, I thought to myself, then count me in as a member of the pauper's club.

"We are going to have your recorded confession typed up for you to sign. Again, do you want your attorney to review it before you sign it?"

"As I said before, that ship has sailed, so no."

He was taken away to be processed with no sign of regret for the killing of his wife, but rather with pride in the clever science problem he had solved.

We reviewed all the evidence. It was Nathan who asked, "Why didn't he just buy an extra life vest, hide it somewhere on board and then swap it at his leisure? He could then dispose of the doctored one in his own good time."

"Maybe," mused the assistant district attorney, "he was afraid that someone would find the extra one before he could get rid of it."

"Good job he didn't," I added. "Otherwise we would never have seen the additional thread and have known that the life verst had been tampered with."

I left the police station after a round of mutual congratulations. Once in the car, I phoned Josie Pedersen. "We brought him in, showed him the evidence, and we have a full confession."

There was something that kept nagging at me. Something was off, but I couldn't place it. Broadmoors confession certainly explained everything.

I called detective Sharrow and told him of my discomfort.

"Cut it out, John, we have our guy."

It then hit me like a ton of bricks.

"Ok, explain this to me. Why did Broadmoor's son hide his face when buying the thread?"

"He's camera shy? Look if you want to go off on a wild goose chase when the goose is already cooked, be my guest."

I realized I had two tasks, the first being to talk to the Marshalls.

It took me a couple of days, but I finally had it. I called Sharrow.

"Ok, John, are you going to ruin a perfectly good confession?"

"Yes, I am. The killing was done by the younger son."

"No way. The father, Michael knew everything."

"That's because he thought the boys were doing a project, so he guided them with the research."

I then went on to tell him that on the day of the killing, the younger son, Doug, was to go sailing with the Marshalls.

Twain Marshall told me, "I remember it well as it was unusual that only Doug was there. The boys were always together, but this time Doug was on his own as his older brother Kent was away at camp."

He went on, "Just as we were about to leave, Doug got a call on his cell phone. He apologized to Michael, told him one of his friends had an emergency, and ran off the boat."

Sharrow's condescending smile slipped a little.

"And then there's the lab notebooks."

"What about them?"

"You notice every page is signed. I didn't pick it up at first as the handwriting is similar on every page. It looks like Doug's handwriting is very similar to his father's."

"Yeah, but so what?"

"It gets better. Like good scientists, the boys signed every page of the lab notebooks for their experiments."

I pulled out copies of the lab notebook pages showing him the initials KB and DB on the life vest experiments and not of MB, Michael Broadmoor's."

"Broadmoor would have looked at the notebooks and have been aware of the experiments. It also explains the son hiding his face when he was buying the thread. That was the thing that got me doubting that Michael Broadmoor was the killer."

"How did Mrs. Broadmoor choose the doctored life vest?"

"An excellent question. I asked the Marshalls why Mrs. Broadmoor was wearing that particular life vest. They told me that Doug went over to his mother and said, 'Here you go mom.' So there's your answer."

"What about fingerprints on the doctored life vest?"

"Why ask me. Isn't that your area as the police? However, I will speculate that there will be some smaller fingerprints that will match both boys."

"Fuck and double fuck. So, Michael Broadmoor was covering for his son or sons."

"I believe that Michael Broadmoor, thought that the whole thing was an intellectual exercise."

"He immediately knew what his son had done when he found that his wife had drowned."

"Exactly."

Michael Broadmoor kept insisting that he was the one who had done the killing but broke down when he saw all the evidence and arranged for a top attorney to defend his son.

They brought Doug Broadmoor in for

questioning that afternoon. He readily admitted all of the evidence was correct and that he had tampered with the life vest. He showed no emotion throughout the interview. When asked why he answered, "The experiment went perfectly." Not a trace of remorse or any other emotion.

I called Josie and told her the sad news: it was her nephew and not her brother-in-law who was responsible for the killing.

There was a long silence. It sounded as if she was crying. In a broken voice, she thanked me. "Goodbye John, I will be eternally grateful to you."

Early Friday morning Juliette and I left the Beverly Hilton where the studio had booked her a room.

"Why don't you stay with me instead of at the hotel?" I asked her.

"It's studio procedure, besides I like being pampered."

At the last minute, we decided to pass on the wine country and instead spend the weekend in San Francisco. I had booked a Metropolitan corner suite at the St. Regis hotel.

"Chérie, that is very expensive."
"It's a celebration. A weekend with you and solving a crime. Besides that, my client, Josie Pedersen, gave me a very generous bonus."

Josie had told me, "I got all this money from my sister's death. The least I can do is to give extra thanks reward to the person who solved her murder."

We pulled onto Santa Monica Boulevard and headed west until we reached the Pacific Coast Highway. We decided to take the leisurely and scenic route up the Pacific Coast Highway. With the top down, we drove north, in the opposite direction of the rush hour traffic heading into town.

We stopped for lunch. Juliette had chosen the Fat Cats Café north of Pismo Beach for lunch.

"I fancied a diner and loved the name."

Because we had a big breakfast before leaving the Hilton, we shared lobster tacos and wine, my wine a small one as I was driving.

When I turned on the security on the car there was a brief flash.

"What was that?" asked Juliette.

"Shake the car," I told her.

She did, and the strobe light started to flash. I showed her the message on my phone "alarm activated."

"That is brilliant."

I told her about Brendan and his friend and how they did this for extra cash.

"I wish cars in Paris had this; it would cut down on all the car alarm noise."

"That is the idea, plus it is personalized."

We got to the St. Regis late afternoon. The car was whisked away by the valet, and a butler took us up to the suite and showed us around. He even had his own phone extension. "Whatever you need, day or night, call this number."

He left us cradled in the lap of luxury.

After we had relaxed from the drive, I suggested to Juliette that I would talk to the concierge about booking dinner for two at a fancy restaurant.

"No Chérie, fancy is what we do in Paris. How about an Indian restaurant?" She knew my passion for Indian cuisine and had come to like it herself.

"Don't you have Indian restaurants in Paris?"

"Yes, I don't know why, but the Indian food in Paris is not quite the same. Of course, the best Indian food in the world is in the UK."

"Better than India," I teased her.

"Yes, even better than India."

"I didn't know that you had been there."

"A lady has to keep a few secrets," she said, giving me a peck on my cheek.

Around eight, we strolled to the nearby

Amber Indian restaurant. Starting with the ubiquitous Samosas, Juliette then wolfed down the Seabass. I had my favorite, Lamb Vindaloo.

We washed down everything with copious amounts of the Haywards 5000 beer. Good job that the hotel was close by as we were weaving side to side across the sidewalk.

The next day we were complete tourists. We walked across the Golden Gate Bridge but Ubered back. We rode cable cars and had lunch at Fisherman's Wharf. After that, we took the Alcatraz tour, and spent time in Union Square. We saved Chinatown for that evening. On the way to Alcatraz, Juliette received a text.

"*Merde*. Sorry Chéri but I have to go back to Paris on Sunday, not Monday."
"We have to leave now, or at the crack of dawn to get you back to LA for your flight."

"Not so fast." Juliette then dialed the Air France first-class desk.

"No problem Miss McKintosh, we have you on the 16.25 out of San Francisco on Sunday afternoon. Seat 3A."

Such a simple solution. Why didn't I think of that?

Sunday saw us getting up late. We asked the concierge if he could recommend a good brunch place.

He suggested Zazie a French Bistro Café, and he wasn't wrong.

"Is it too French for you?" I asked Juliette.

"*Mais non,*" she replied.

We both had Eggs Benedict washed down with copious amounts of coffee, mine Pierre Noir, hers St. Trop.

At 2.30 p.m. I dropped her off at International Departures at The San Francisco airport. We hugged and reluctantly parted with a chorus of "see you soon."

I kept going south on the 101 and got back to Los Angeles late Sunday night.

I met with Issy and CT at the Culver City Starbucks. I gave each of them an envelope. Inside each, a check for $10,000.00.

I had given Dolores a similar check early that morning. Their eyes widened, and I swear Issy went pale.

"Who do we have to kill for you?" they asked in unison.

"No one. The bonus is courtesy of our client who wanted to show her gratitude for solving her sister's murder. As you two did a lot of the work which helped solve this crime, I thought it only fair that you received some of the bonus."

"The main reason I wanted to meet with the two of you is that I am going to be in Paris with

Juliette for three months."

"Wow in Paris? Congratulations!"

"Yes, that's where she lives. I already talked to Dolores. She'll say that I am out of town for a few days and can meet with the client by phone or video link. I would like the two of you to do the usual low-level searches and be available for anything important on a priority basis. If you are doing a visual inspection of a crime scene, we can use zoom or WhatsApp. For interviews, you can use an audio feature on your phone so I can listen in."

They both nodded their agreement.

"When are you off?" asked Issy.

"This weekend."

THE END